FISHING FOR LUCK

Murray Richter

Lucky Reader Books LLC
Dallas, TX

Published by Lucky Reader Books LLC
3010 LBJ Freeway Suite 1200, Dallas, TX 75234

ISBN-13: 978-1-7364895-0-5

Cover design by Nathan Reinhardt
http://nathanr.carbonmade.com/

First edition: May, 2021

Summary: Seventh-grader Kevin's plans for a perfect spring break are shattered by the return of an unpleasant part of his past.

Thank you for purchasing this Lucky Reader Books LLC publication.
www.luckyreaderbooksllc.com

In memory and appreciation of
John "Don Juan" Argubright,
a fantastic brother-in-law and an amazing person.
Thank you for making the world a better place.

CHAPTER 1

"Will it survive an attack from a forty-pound catfish?" I asked, eyeing the massive wooden raft in my best friend Preech's front yard.

He laughed. "You bet, Kev. I used the finest lumber I could find at the dump and painted each board thirteen times before screwin' 'em together."

"What about snakes?"

Preech tapped the sharpened broomsticks poking out from the sides of the raft, which was about the size of four teachers' desks combined. "Check those out. By my calculations, there's no way the slithering serpents can make it past that kind of defense."

I touched one of the points and checked my finger for blood. "Excellent. What's that in the middle?"

"Trap door."

"What for?"

"In case a flock of bloodthirsty parakeets or rabid bats attack and try to rip us to pieces. Now we've got an escape route."

"Awesome. You thought of everything." I gave him a high five. "This'll be the best spring break ever."

"I hope so." Preech scratched his chin. "The only worry I've got is if it'll carry us back from the island once we load up with a bunch of whoppers."

"Thanks again, amigo. Gotta be tons of fish out there," I tried to stop a yawn, but couldn't.

His eyebrows shot up and down. "What's the matter? Couldn't sleep knowing you'll probably be the first seventh grader ever to catch a state-record catfish?"

"Nah, I wish. My folks were fighting again last night. Got so loud, it upset Milly. I can't remember how many books I had to read before she finally crashed."

Milly was my little sister and had two speeds: asleep and a hundred miles an hour.

"Why were they fighting?" Preech asked.

"Dude, I don't know. Got a weird feeling it's something I did."

"How could it be you? Did you ask them what's up?"

"No way," I said shaking my head, thinking how extremely uncomfortable I got talking to grown-ups about that kind of stuff. Like licking my own elbow, dancing in front of anyone, or swimming up a waterfall—never gonna happen.

"Why not? May be something totally different." He spread his arms out at the neat piles of sprockets, gizmos, tubes, and what appeared to be robot guts scattered around his yard. I figured he had everything he needed to build a rocket to Mars. And if anyone could, Preech was the guy. "I just don't have a lot of time for drama like that," Preech said. "What keeps me busy are my inventions and thinking up new ways to prank Rudy." He looked at his watch. "Who's late, by the way."

I checked mine. "Huh, he's never late."

Preech shrugged. "That knucklehead probably found something dead and spent the last half hour poking it with a stick." He snapped his fingers. "Think I'll give the wagon wheels one last greasing with the brand-new super-grease I invented."

Three little red wagons squatted under the raft. "What happened to the handles?"

Preech jogged to the garage. "Took 'em off for a place to tie off on our bikes."

I pulled on the rope that crisscrossed the raft and secured it to the wagons, it was so tight it snapped when I let go. Preech returned with a coffee can full of goop the color of blended catfish skins. He grabbed a stick off the ground to stir the gooey concoction and climbed under the raft.

I pinched my nose shut as a sharp chemical twang filled the yard. "What's in that?"

"A highly volatile mixture of every grease we had, plus some goose grease, baby oil, some of my mom's face cream, butter, and anything else slippery I could find." His head popped out from under the raft. "Remember when The Oracle taught us to shoot bows and arrows?"

The Oracle was Preech's uncle Oliver, a name we gave him because he was quite possibly the smartest and coolest guy on the planet. But we never called him that to his face. Even though the name sounded respectful, we'd never do anything to disrespect a real-life Army hero.

"Yep."

Preech slid his finger down the side of his nose. "And remember he showed us there's always a little grease here to put on the bow rest to keep from making noise when you pull the arrow back?"

I nodded.

"Well, I've been scraping mine off every night for a month and mixed some in there, too. This could be the slickest stuff on the planet." He disappeared back under the raft.

"Excellent," I said. "Did The Oracle come back from Germany?"

"Got in last night."

"Any luck finding her?"

"Nope." Preech's muffled voice floated up from under the raft. "Three trips over there so far and still no luck. What amazes me is that a few months ago, he didn't even know she was alive. That he still had a wife after all these years. Man, war sure can mess things up."

"We're heading to his place tomorrow, right?" A tingle of excitement rippled through me. I loved everything about The Oracle's ranch, except for Pele, the donkey. That evil beast could kick somebody into next month.

"Yep. And he said there may be some good news about our lucky rocks."

I dug mine out of my pocket. "If these turn out to be real diamonds, what are you gonna do with the cash?"

He laughed. "Got some epic ideas for pranks on Rudy that'll be costly, but definitely worth the money. And I'd like to finance a trip back to Florida and dive that shipwreck again. Think I saw a bunch more lucky rocks scattered around, right before that gargantuan shark cut our time short. What would you buy?"

Pictures of a real-live fishing boat and new rods and reels floated around my head, but disappeared when I thought about my parents. Their fight was definitely about money. Would I have to give them some? All of it, maybe?

"Not sure yet," I said. "It'll be good to see The Oracle again. It's always fun at his place."

"Heck yeah," answered Preech. "Hey, you should ask him what to do about your folks."

"I don't know. Wouldn't want to drag him into anything."

"If anyone can help, he can. And like he says, 'Things aren't always as they appear.'"

I slid the sparkly stone back into my pocket. "We'll see."

"Ready to rock and roll." Preech wiggled out from under the raft, stuck the stick in the grease, and jogged to the garage.

My other best friend, Rudy, came flying down the street, pumping his pedals like a pack of wolves was after him. He came to a screeching sideways stop, creating a long, black, swooping skid mark on the driveway shaped like a giant fishhook. Rudy wiped the sweat off his forehead on his shirt sleeve.

"Morning, Big Cat," I said.

"Morning, Kev. Sorry I'm late. Where's Dog Breath?"

"I'm in the garage, you big galoot. Just like a blister, you show up when all the work's done. I was five minutes away from seeing if Kev wanted to head to the pond without you so we could—" As Preech walked out, he glanced at Rudy and started laughing so hard he had to bend over to catch his breath. "What's up with your hair? Ride your bike through a car wash?"

Rudy licked his palm and ran it over his head. "Aww man, nope. Didn't have time to shower. Me and Mom were watching the news." His eyes bugged out. "Did y'all hear?"

Preech smiled. "That the circus is back in town? And they picked you for the freak show?"

"No, Weasel Face. They were taking a busload of prisoners from here to a different jail, and the bus drove off the bridge into the river." Rudy smacked his palm with his fist. "Hit so hard the bus split open like a banana. Found all but a couple of the bodies. Said they probably got washed down-river and are fish food by now."

Rudy's head swiveled back and forth from me to Preech. "I kept watching to see if they'd name names of people on the bus, but they didn't."

The spit in my mouth dried up. "Y'all think Ted was on the bus?"

Rudy nodded. "Yep. Never thought I'd have to think about the meanest stepdad in the history of stepdads ever again, but the guy on the news said all the prisoners were on board."

We didn't blink or breathe for a whole minute. Pictures zipped through my head: Ted screaming at Rudy, my lucky rock slicing his head open, and the police throwing Ted into their cruiser.

Preech waved his hands in the air. "I read somewhere that 86.7 percent of what people worry about never even happens."

I gulped. "You know, I've always wondered if he'd bust out and come after me for nailing him."

Rudy shrugged. "Wasn't like he was on his way to being an underwear model or anything. That gash probably made him look better."

Preech wrapped his arm around my shoulder. "C'mon, guys, gotta be a sixty-foot drop from that bridge. No way anyone survived. And I'm not going to let some what-ifs ruin the day that we're gonna catch some monsters. People will forever remember the year 1980 and will weep and gnash their teeth that bigger fish will never be caught."

Rudy's stomach growled so loud I jumped. "Man, forgot breakfast too. Y'all got any chow?"

Preech shook his head. "All you do is eat. I might have peanuts or something in my backpack."

Rudy puffed out his chest. "All I do is eat because I'm gonna grow up and be super strong and fast. You know, a man's man, like Paul Bunyan, or the Flash."

Preech hooked his thumb at me. "Nobody can run as fast as Kev did the day Milly broke her arm and he ran her to the hospital. The dude only had a block head start, and I still couldn't catch him on my bike."

"Crazy day," I said.

Rudy whistled and rubbed the raft. "Looks cool. Will it float?"

"Yes, Brainless Wonder. And take a full-on assault from a gator if there are any in the pond. Daylight's a burnin', so we gotta get the show on the road if we're going to have any time to fish the island."

Preech ran back into the garage, and came back with a pool cue. "Last thing we've got to do is make the pull ropes. They have to be the *exact* same length."

He laid the stick on the ground, looped the rope two times next to it, and took his pocket knife out of his backpack. After cutting the pieces, Preech stood up, held them next to each other, and nodded. "Pull your bikes over there and I'll tie one end to a wagon and the other under your bike seat."

Rudy laughed. "Something's been bugging me about your bike. I just figured out that there's not a pile of junk pokin' out all around it. Looks naked."

Preech let out a long breath as he climbed under the raft. "Well, El Dunderhead, I have meticulously combed over every piece of this plan. I don't want anything messing up Kev's chance of catching the biggest catfish in Texas today."

"Thanks, bro. What can I do to help?"

"Just put your bike on the left, or port side, Rudy's bike in the middle, and mine on the right, or starboard side. Hey, did y'all know the starboard side is on the right because that was the side the plank was normally on pirate ships? Astronomers would also use it to get away from the candlelight on the boat to study stars and stuff."

Rudy grinned at me and rolled his eyes. "Whatever, Word Nerd. Didn't you say we gotta boogie?"

"Done," Preech said. He climbed out from under the raft, tied off our bikes, and jumped on his. "Let's roll."

My leg muscles burned and the wagon wheels squealed in protest as the massive wooden beast lurched forward and followed us out of the yard.

"Awesome," said Preech. "Let's move at the same pace, and we should have plenty of time to figure out how to get to the island."

Rudy pumped his pedals. "Figure out how to get to the island?"

"Well, I didn't have time to carve any paddles, so we can cut some cane to use as push poles to—" Preech's head whipped around to look at the raft. "Aww, man. I forgot all of our gear and stuff. We gotta go back."

"Smooth move, Ex-Lax." Rudy stopped pedaling.

"Great Caesar's ghost!" Preech yelled. "Don't do that; don't stop pedaling. Oh man, oh man, I just realized a major hole in my plan." The color drained out of Preech's face, and his eyelid geared up for maximum twitch mode: a sure sign he was about to freak out.

I pointed to where the street ended. "No problem, buddy. We'll stop up there, unhook the raft, and go back and grab everything."

"That's the problem," croaked Preech. "We can't...we can't stop. We literally cannot stop. If we do, we'll be skewered like shish-kabobs!"

CHAPTER 2

Rudy jerked on the rope under his seat. "Dude, untie this sucker or cut me loose. Now!"

"No can do," hollered Preech. "I did, like, six hitch knots and some other ones I learned from the Boy Scout Handbook. Knife's in my backpack."

I stared at the stop sign coming at us and then at the trees across the street. We were so close I could almost count the leaves. "Can we hop the curb and ride into the forest?"

Preech shook his head. "Nope, trees are too close together and too many cactuses. Gotta go left."

"Left?" Rudy yelled. "That's the wrong way!"

"It's statistically impossible for all three stoplights to be green if we go through town, and there's cars and people and ladies with baby strollers and stuff." Preech jumped on his pedals. "We have to time this perfectly. Turn as hard as you can when we're close and hammer down."

We reached the end of the street. I closed my eyes, jammed my handlebars to the left, and pedaled harder than I ever had.

My bike shuddered, the wagon wheels screamed, and it felt like my spine got ripped backwards and a load of barf was about to go frontwards.

Preech hollered, "Go! Go! Go!" and my eyes flew open.

We'd somehow made the turn. The ropes snapped tight, and I glanced back at the raft.

What I saw was a beast coming after us with an evil grin, full of needle-sharp teeth thirsty for boy blood.

"Okay, okay, fellas," Preech whimpered, "gain enough speed to keep a little slack in the lines and everything should be fine. Just fine. Takin' the back roads puts us at the pond around sunset, and I'll have ten plans to fix this by the time we get there. Maybe more."

The pavement beneath us ended, the hard-packed dirt road began, and we pedaled.

I'd ridden with my dad in his truck a ton of times down those roads, and normally I would try to guess how many quail or rattlesnakes were in the trees and brush that separated the huge farms. We cruised by them, and I wondered if an oak would give you two coffins or three.

Rudy called Preech every cuss word I'd ever heard, plus a couple of new ones.

I said, "Hey, buddy, what if we start going slower and slower? It'll just stop, right?"

Preech shook his head. "Nah. Good thinking, Kev, but I thought of that, too. Since I re-greased the wheels so good, this bad boy will not slow down or stop...ever." He pointed his chin ahead of us. "We gotta take this road."

"You sure?" Rudy asked.

Preech nodded and stood on his pedals. "Same as before, turn your handlebars and pedal harder than you ever have."

I cranked my handlebars hard right and pumped the pedals with everything I had.

"Uh, oh," Preech wheezed. "Oh, no."

I looked up. The weeds in the bar ditch had disappeared, and I saw our postman, Mr. Bernard, standing next to his jeep in front of the little house on the corner.

"Look out!" I screamed.

"Outta the way!" Rudy yelled.

"Save yourself, man!" Preech hollered.

Mr. Bernard's eyes bugged out. Letters scattered like doves as he jumped into his vehicle.

Preech's chin was on his shoulder. "Miss it, miss it, miss it."

The rolling ship of pain skipped and slid sideways. Like taking a bite out of a doughnut, the very last spear ripped a huge gash in Mr. Bernard's front tire.

He jumped out, shook his fists, and over the squeaky wagon wheels yelled, "Back here, boys. Now!"

Preech yelled back, "Oh, my gosh, so sorry, sir! We'd stop if we could! I'll fix the tire, I promise! So sorry!"

The killer raft creaked behind us. We continued on possibly our last bike ride ever.

"Not good, not good at all," whimpered Preech. "Destruction of government property. That's a felony, I think."

Rudy chewed his lip. "This is so messed up."

Preech cleared his throat. "Speaking of getting messed up, and specifically wanting to avoid that, I think I've figured out our exit strategy once we reach the pond."

Rudy stared ahead. "Whatcha got, Alfred Einstein?"

Preech pointed his fingers straight out and tilted his elbow up. "There's quite a sharp decline as we approach the pond, correct?"

"Yeah," answered Rudy.

"So, we use gravity to our advantage. Kev, as soon as we get close to the big rocks by the water, turn hard left and jump off your bike, okay?"

I nodded.

Preech gave me a quick thumbs-up. "Good. I'll do the same, but to the starboard side. I figure the ropes tied to us are *almost* long enough to reach past the spears, so a good sideways jump should do the trick."

We rode for a bit. I tried to wrap my head around the plan.

"Umm, what about me?" Rudy asked.

"Oh yeah, that. You're the fortunate one, my friend. You have options."

"Options?"

Preech nodded. "Yes, yes, you lucky duck. You can choose to either jump frontwards into the water *or* backwards onto the raft."

Rudy gritted his teeth. "I don't think 'lucky' is the right word."

"Options are fantastic. Plus, girls dig scars."

"A minute ago, you said we can't jump back because if we didn't go high enough, it'd rip our guts out and—"

"Oh no, no, that was for me and Kev. You, however, have more muscles in one leg than most people have in their whole body. Out of the three of us, you have the best statistical chance of living through something like that."

"You know you're dead if we do live through this, right?" Rudy said.

Preech gulped.

We survived the rest of the way, and the glorious shine on the pond appeared. There were fish swirls everywhere, like God had dropped a handful of cannonballs into the water.

Pedaling fast, we flew down the incline leading to the pond, barely able to keep ahead of the killer raft. I looked down and then shot upright in my seat.

I whistled at Preech. "Dude, this is bad. Way, way bad. My shoelace came undone. Totally wrapped around the pedal!"

His head jerked up and down, trying to get a look around Rudy. "Can you pull your foot out?" screamed Preech.

I lifted my leg, making my brakes engage and the raft surge closer like it was trying to lick my back tire. I shook my head.

Preech jabbed his finger at the ground. "Okay, the rope may be long enough to reach outside the spears. If not, get as low as you can, to go under them, alright?"

The pond flew at us with every blink. My heart thumped so hard I thought it was going to climb up my throat.

Rudy slid his feet onto the long metal tube that connected the handlebars to the rest of his bike. He glanced back at me and nodded. His mouth said, "We got this, buddy." But his eyes said, "Man, this is gonna hurt."

"Go time. *Now!*" Preech yelled.

I cranked my handlebars hard left, laid my bike over, and shut my eyes right before my head slammed into a greenish-brown blur of weeds and dirt. I skidded on my back, waiting for the spears to slice through me when my shoe popped off and I slid to a stop.

Through the dust cloud I saw that Rudy had made the jump onto the ship of death. He looked like a human-sized tick with his fingernails dug into the wood.

The raft smacked into the rocks next to the pond with a loud, metallic crunch. It groaned and flipped up, catapulting Rudy over the water.

"Oooooh," I said. He flew like an angel, and then tucked like a turtle right before he splashed down.

The raft hit with a deafening smack, and a mini tidal wave cruised across the pond. The wagon wheels looked like spines on the Loch Ness Monster's back as they bobbed and bucked in the water.

Over the ringing in my ears, I heard Preech holler, "Yes, yes, yes!" He was doing his victory dance, his fingers pointed like V's to the sky while he jumped around in a circle.

He ran over, pulled me to my feet, hugged me, and hummed "We Are the Champions" by Queen. Dirt and pebbles peppered his teeth. "You okay, Kev?"

"Think so."

Rudy was dog paddling with one arm, pointing at Preech with the other. "You are so dead."

Preech jumped behind me. "Now, now, not so fast," he yelled back. "What you experienced was a once-in-a-lifetime *event*! People would pay good money for that at Six Flags."

Rudy shook his head.

Preech laughed. "And if you don't pound me, I'll waive the fee for your ride. Plus, you got a shower out of the deal. For free."

Rudy smiled. "Dude, that was nuts."

Preech pointed at my bike, and then at his. "Hey, looks like they're okay."

Our bikes were nestled in the rocks on the bank, the ropes tethering them to the wagons.

"Uh oh." He looked at Rudy's. Both tires were bent like tacos, and the handlebars were twisted backwards.

Rudy got to the shallows and stomped out.

"Hey, Big Guy." Preech gulped. "Appears there was a minor technical difficulty with your bike. But don't worry, I'll fix things lickety-split."

Staring at his bike, Rudy flicked a piece of algae off his finger onto Preech's face. "Oh, yes, you will."

Most of the remaining daylight slipped away as we unsnarled Preech's amazingly tight balls of knots. With no knives, we had to use our teeth and sticks to undo them and separate the wagons from the raft.

"Hey," Preech said, coiling the rope in his hand, "check out the hollowed-out tree trunk over there. Let's use that as a hidey-hole until we establish an operational base on the island." He set the rope in the stump and slid a flat rock the size of a manhole cover on top.

I fingered the small piece of shoelace twisted around my bike pedal. "Do y'all know where my shoe went?"

Preech looked at the pedal and in the weeds and water. "Whoa, must've been violent. Gettin' dark; we'll look tomorrow when we come back."

I nodded.

Preech shrugged. "Bummer you gotta walk back, Rudinator. Good news is your football legs will grow strong like a big ole bull's."

Rudy grabbed Preech's handlebars. "Nope, I'll be taking yours, thank you very much." His eyes lit up. "Or even better..." He tapped the wagon tied to Preech's bike. "I'll ride back in style. To even the score after you almost got me killed fifteen times today."

Preech coughed and sputtered. "What?"

Rudy climbed into the wagon. With his arms and legs spilling out everywhere, he looked like a GI Joe doll in a matchbox.

I put Rudy's pretzel-like bike in the other wagon and tied it to mine. "Got yours, Big Cat. What should we do with the one that got all busted up?"

"The amazing thing about today," Preech grinned, "is that the only casualties were one wagon and one bike. I say leave it for now. Would be smart to have something here to cannibalize for parts if we need to down the road."

Rudy smiled and laced his fingers behind his head. "Mush, dog boy, mush."

We got to the top of the hill. Sweat poured off of Preech, and he wheezed like my aunt who smoked three packs of cigarettes a day.

"Hey, bud, do you think we'll get in trouble for Mr. Bernard's Jeep?" I asked.

Preech slapped his forehead. "Glad you reminded me."

Rudy's voice pierced the air. "Dude, I am not going down for that. Mom says if I ever go to jail, she'll visit, but she'll bring a Bible and either hand it to me or throw it at me depending on what I did."

Preech stopped, struggling to catch his breath. "No worries, gents, we're safe as kittens. Once I fix Mr. Bernard's tire and ask Mom to bake him some cookies, I'll give him the prototype whistle I modified to repel dogs." He tapped his chin. "I'll make sure to not give him the one I engineered to *attract* dogs. That could end poorly."

We rolled down the hard-packed dirt roads, and once we hit the asphalt, Preech put his finger to his lips and grinned at a huge pothole ahead of us.

He eased around the massive hole, and then took off.

The wagon halfway disappeared into the crater. Rudy was suspended in midair for a second, and then he slammed back into it. He was barely able to pull himself into his tiny metal chariot as it clawed its way back onto the road. "Dangit, watch where you're going. I almost bit my tongue off!"

Preech grinned. "Whoops, that sucker snuck up on me. Gettin' dark, but I'll keep an eye out." He looked at me and whispered, "Speaking of not biting your tongue, you gonna talk to your folks tonight?"

I squirmed on my bike seat. "We'll see. Maybe things will be alright by the time I get home." The words felt as hollow as The Oracle's fake leg he got fighting the bad guys in the war.

Preech snapped his fingers. "Hey, we gotta be at Uncle Oliver's ranch at the crack of dawn tomorrow, so we'll shift the fishing trip to the afternoon."

I eased to a stop. "Okay. Gonna ride the alleys the rest of the way home. Want me to take this wagon with me?"

"Nah," Preech said. "Let's attach that one behind the lounging Yeti. I need to inspect and re-grease the wheels before I get going on fixing his bike."

I tied the other wagon off, getting it as close as possible to give Rudy a kind of footrest.

His teeth glowed in the moonlight. "Thanks, bro."

"*Hasta manana*, dudes." I pedaled away, imagining every step I was going to take the next day to battle and drag in a catfish as big as a Volkswagen.

Cruising up to the gate for my backyard, I slammed into a tree limb. My bike slid out from under me and smashed into our trashcans as my head bounced off of the hard-packed alley dirt.

The stars stopped spinning, and I realized what I hit wasn't a tree limb.

It was an arm, attached to a man with a big, ugly, nasty scar.

CHAPTER 3

Sweat came so fast I thought it was going to squirt out of my forehead. I blinked hard and wondered if I was seeing things. "T-T-Ted?"

"Where you been, punk?"

I couldn't breathe. "What're you doing here?"

He lurched out of the shadows, grabbed my leg, and pulled his face an inch away from mine. "Lookin' fer you. You're gonna help Ted clear his name."

The rotten vomit smell of his breath made my stomach ball into knots. I pointed to myself. "Who? Me?"

He pulled me up by my shirt.

"Gaaah!" I said, looking at one of the grossest things I'd ever seen. "Whoa, Ted, what happened? You got a lump the size of a softball."

He let go and twisted his head towards me. "What? Am I bleedin'?"

The bulge pulsed like it had a heartbeat of its own. It was a disgusting purplish-red color, like a pile of catfish guts.

I turned to run. "Gonna go call the doctor."

Ted grabbed my arm and spun me around. "Shut up. No sawbones." A wicked grin slid across his face. "Couple of days ago, the fella who runs the dumpy little grocery store in The Flats got thrown in with us, something about a card game gone wrong. Blood got spilled."

Everything suddenly went into slow motion. He'd found out.

Ted coughed, winced, and took a deep breath. "We got to talkin' about my wrongful imprisonment. He told me about a fake letter full of lies about me he seen exactly like the one that railroaded me into jail. And the dangedest thing? The kid that picked it up sounded like the spittin' image of Rudy."

His eyes turned to slits. "You know anything about that?"

Know anything? Of course I did—I was there. My mouth went so dry it felt like I'd swallowed a gallon of dirt.

A mini movie from that day at Rudy's house rolled through my head: The mostly empty bottle of whiskey in Ted's hand, the waterfall of blood that spewed from his head after my lucky rock laid it open, the officer's nightstick knocking Ted out, Rudy cramming the fake letter in Ted's back pocket, the tears on Rudy and his mom's faces lit up red and blue by the police cruiser hauling Ted away.

He coughed, winced again, and spit through clenched teeth. "The guards won't listen to a word I say, and my good-fer-nuthin' lawyer ain't calling me back. Got half a mind to go to the cops and tell them myself, but figure I need to scrub off them other lies they got pinned on me first. Was gonna hunt Rudy down and beat the truth outta him, but since I'm laid up a bit, you're gonna help ole Ted make things straight."

I gulped.

He pointed towards my home. "Need a place to hole up, 'til things get figured out."

Pictures of Milly, Mom, and Dad flashed through my mind. I thought fast. "Umm, sorry, sir, we don't have an extra room."

"What you gonna do about that?"

Every atom in my body begged me to scream or run or both. But the look in his eyes told me I'd regret it. I looked at his arm and figured out what had been causing a clicking noise that had been driving me crazy. "What's that?"

He fingered the short chain attached to the handcuff on his wrist, surprised it was there. "Huh, looks like you gotta find me a hacksaw, too."

The word "saw" triggered something in my brain, giving me a seed of hope. "What about Old Man Perkins' place?" I asked.

Ted nodded, and then slowly shook his head. "Nah, stupid idea. Didn't something bad happen out there?"

"Not that I know of," which was *kind of* the truth. Some people say Old Man Perkins murdered his family and ran away. Others say he got a job in Florida, and they just up and moved.

I pictured him getting terrorized by ghosts, and the hope grew. "Could be a good place to lie low while things get figured out. Nobody ever goes out there, sir."

Ted stepped towards me. His foot skidded sideways and slid out from under him. "Dang, near twisted my ankle off." Ted grabbed something off the ground, got on his feet, and wound up like a baseball pitcher about to chunk it down the alley. He paused. "Well, well, looky here." His eyebrows danced up and down. In a creepy kid's voice, he said, "Finders keepers."

I jammed my hand in my pocket—empty. A new wave of terror lit me up as I watched my lucky rock twist between his grimy fingers. I opened my palm. "Oh hey, Ted, sir, umm, uhh, that's mine. Must've fallen out of my pocket when I wiped out."

Ted held it up to the moonlight. "That maggot Rudy was always squawking about y'all finding them and how much money you were going to get. These real?"

What was unreal was watching him hold the actual thing I'd used to help take him down.

"The guy that owns the jewelry store has been out of town for a while; Africa someone said. When he gets back, we'll let him take a look." I held out my hand again. "Once I find out, I'll let you know, sir."

Ted snorted. "Nope. You don't exactly strike me as too keen on helping Ted with what he needs, so I reckon I'll keep this little nugget to be my insurance policy to make sure you do."

He slid my lucky rock into his shirt pocket and stepped into the lamplight. I noticed his clothes. Belly fat and hair poked out of the holes in his shirt that was way too little. His pants were at least three sizes too small, complete with a belt made out of rope. And he was barefoot. Ted looked like he'd mugged a scarecrow.

He snapped his fingers. "Listen, boy, you gotta find me some shoes. And whiskey."

"Umm, okay, Ted, sir," I said. "I'll see what I can do. But my folks keep the whiskey locked up." *Like you should be,* I thought.

"Need some shoes. Gimme yours." He glanced at my feet and frowned. "Only one? You're already lettin' me down, runt."

It took me a second to remember what had happened at the pond. I peeled off my shoe. "Here you go, sir."

He wrestled it on. His toes were balled up and bulging in the front of the shoe, begging to escape.

"The way I figure," Ted said, "forgin' government documents is big-time crime. The feds wouldn't think twice about sending a kid up the river for something like that. They got a couple of other lies stuck on me, but I can work on gettin' those put to rest once I'm cleared on that letter. What I can't figure is why he done what he did. With me being a perfect daddy and all."

A perfect daddy doesn't give his wife and stepson matching black eyes, I thought. But I didn't dare say a word.

Ted blew his nose in his hand and wiped it on his shirt. "Maybe you ain't as dumb as you look. Think I'll hole up at Old Man Perkins' for a bit. Now go. Got ten minutes to fetch me what I need for out there."

I started for my house. He snapped his fingers. "Oh, and looky here, boy."

I turned around.

He patted his pocket. "If I so much as hear a cop or see anyone but *you* around here, I will make sure this disappears for good. And I'll thump you so hard your kids'll be born dizzy. Understood?"

I could barely catch what he said over my heartbeat roaring in my ears. "Yes, sir."

"And another thing, I recall Rudy sayin' you got a little sister. Sure would be a shame if bad fortune fell on her because you didn't do as told, don't you think?"

Unable to take a breath, I nodded and eased my bike through the gate. For the first time ever, I locked it.

CHAPTER 4

How can this be happening? Why me? I pushed my bike around the mesquite trees, instead of under them so my tires and feet wouldn't pick up any thorns.

What if I told someone? They'd say "Call the police." What would the police do? Do an investigation. What was Preech's "word of the day" a couple of weeks ago? Accomplish? No, the word was accomplice: a person who helps someone else commit a crime. Me and Preech might get figured as accomplices. Was I old enough to get chunked into juvenile jail? All I'd heard about it was horrible food, constant manual labor, and zero fishing time. I didn't want any part of *that*.

I laid my bike down and stepped through the back door to the garage. Suddenly, a pink blur knocked me sideways.

"Gotcha!" Milly screamed. I caught her in midair, barely able to keep my balance, before crashing against the wall.

"Whoa, wow. Yep, you did. You got me good, Ninja Monkey."

She hugged me with her arms and her legs, picked her head up, and peeked outside. "Who you talking to?"

My eyes shot to the yard, looking everywhere at once. Thankfully, no sign of Ted. I set Milly down then closed and locked the door. "To myself. What are you doing?"

She grinned. "Playing beauty shop."

I glanced at the garage floor and saw a pair of scissors, two heaps of brown and blond hair, and a mountain of bald Barbie dolls.

She picked one up and patted the mangy scalp, like a beaver had chewed its hair off. "When everything grows back, I hope it's curly, don't you?"

A chill ran down my spine as I thought about Ted in the alley fifty steps away, ticking off the minutes with his fingers and toes.

"Yeah, I hope so." The evening air was cool, but my hands were slick with sweat. I pulled the big garage door shut, locked it, and yanked a sleeping bag off the top shelf.

Milly's eyes lit up as she dropped the doll and clapped. "Yes! Woo-hoo! Camping time, like Mom!"

"What?" I asked, trying to find the moldiest and greasiest camping pillow I could out of the pile on the bottom shelf.

"Mom went across town to Aunt Deedee's for a sleepover." Milly spread her arms wide. "She took her great big suitcase; gonna be a long one."

Goosebumps erupted on my arms and neck. "What? When?"

"Today. Sooo, can you read in my room? Mom got me new books."

"Maybe. Where's Dad?"

"Sleeping in the front room."

"Huh? On the couch? Why?"

Milly shrugged. "Dunno. He was super-duper tired. When I asked him to help clean up a bunch of glitter I spilled, he said 'Go play,' so I played beauty shop."

"Okay. Promise me you'll stay right here. I'll check on him and be back in a minute."

She smiled her mile-wide grin, stepped in front of me, and gave a thumbs-up. "Okie dokie. Oh, and your booger holes are clean as a whistle!"

"Umm, thanks?" I said.

She turned and put her fists on her hips to survey the dolls and doll parts scattered across the concrete floor. "Be quick; I need to take my girls inside. The car hole gets pretty drafty."

Mom said Milly would grow out of the stage of naming everything she could after holes, but nobody knew when.

"Okay, stay here for a minute, and I'll help you."

The house was darker than I'd ever seen. Felt weird, like someone, or something, had died. I clicked on the hallway switch, eased the door open, and poked my head into the front room. Light from the porch covered everything with a fuzzy gray fog.

"Pops?"

His head jerked up off the couch. He sniffed. A pillow he'd taken from their bed stuck to his face for a split second, and when it released, I noticed a huge wet spot.

He'd been crying.

"Hey, sport," Dad croaked. His head moved out of the slice of light on his pillow. I couldn't see him, but sensed for one of the first times ever he wasn't smiling.

"Umm, everything alright?"

"Well, to be honest, no, not so much," he said. "We're in a rough spot, champ."

My fingers dug into the sleeping bag and nasty pillow I was hugging. "Is there...? Did I...?" Every speck of air disappeared from my body. It was impossible to push out any words.

Dad sighed. "Uh, well, yeah, I guess you need to know, that—"

Just then, Ted's lumpy Frankenstein head appeared in the window right behind the couch. Dad's words drowned out, and my world kicked into an even faster spin.

CHAPTER 5

I dropped the stuff in my arms and ran into the room. My shins slammed into the table in front of the couch and a sickening crunch echoed off the walls. Light pinged off of Dad's wedding ring as it skidded across the table.

"Whoa, easy there," he said.

A panicked voice screamed in my head, *Why is his ring not on his finger where it's been forever?*

I limped around, sat next to Dad on the couch, reached behind him, and furiously pointed sideways, begging Ted to get out of sight.

He frowned, tapped his wrist like he was wearing a watch, and slowly disappeared, like a crocodile slithering back into an ocean of murky darkness.

"On second thought," Dad said, "I'm worn out." He squeezed my shoulder, stretched out on the couch, and closed his eyes. "We'll talk in the morning, okay?"

"Yes, sir." I stood, picked up the sleeping bag and pillow, eased the door shut, walked out of the house, and crossed the front yard. Ted's voice floated out of my father's truck. "Psst, hey, maggot, go snag me the keys."

My throat began to clamp shut, like I was choking. "What?"

He spoke slowly, as if I was an idiot. "Go. Fetch. Me. The. Keys." Ted pointed at the house. "Now!"

I had to think fast. "I don't know, sir. Do you have your license?"

"You don't need a license to drive. All you need is a key." His eyes were burning mad. "And I'm getting mighty tired of asking." He grabbed the door handle and started to ease out of the truck. "Looks like I gotta get them myself."

I gulped. "A couple of things: Dad needs his truck to go to work, and there's not a garage at Old Man Perkins'. Someone might start poking around if a truck was there all of a sudden."

Ted blinked and did a slow nod. I started to feel a little cocky about my quick thinking.

"Alright then, gimme your bike," he said, and the cockiness disappeared like spit on a griddle. He reached for the sleeping bag and nasty pillow. "What's that?"

"This? The stuff you asked for."

"Food, aspirin, and whiskey is what I asked for." Ted gritted his teeth and slammed his fists on the steering wheel. The clicking noise from his handcuff ricocheted around the inside of the truck. "You're working hard to let me down, punk."

I watched my lucky rock slide back and forth in his pocket. "Okay, sorry, sir, must not have heard you right. Be right back."

I handed him what I had, ran to the house, eased the front door open, and tip-toed to the kitchen pantry. Reaching as far back as I could, I plucked out forgotten cans of Beenie Weenies, Vienna sausages, and green beans. I blew the dust off, found a grocery sack, and set them inside. "Probably older than me, and beggars can't be choosers, you big, weird maniac," I whispered.

Reaching back again, I found a mystery can, thinking a mouse or something had chewed most of the label off. *And your surprise of the day, Ted.*

Turning around to set the can in the sack, I jerked to a stop, almost bonking Milly on the head. She was bent over, looking into it, her arms wrapped around the dolls, both fists full of blond and brown hair.

Baldbie dolls, I thought, which normally would have given me a chuckle, but there was something about having a lumpy-headed lunatic gorilla who might be kicking our front door off its hinges any second that sucked the fun out of the world.

"Yuck," she said, blinking at me. "Is there stuff in the food hole to make s'mores for our camp out?"

"Don't think the camp-out's gonna happen, at least not today, Little Monkey."

"Rats." She turned to leave.

"Hey, would you run real quick and grab me the aspirin from Mom and Dad's bathroom? You know what the bottle looks like?"

Milly nodded. "Yep, yep, Mom ate a bunch of them today."

"Great, thanks. I bet you're so fast I can't even count to ten by the time you're back."

She dumped everything on the floor and bolted out of the kitchen.

I pulled on the liquor cabinet door—locked. Thankful, I said, "No dice on the whiskey, Ted." Food was one thing, but taking liquor felt like something totally different, like stealing.

Milly flew back into the kitchen and handed me the aspirin.

"Thanks, Rocket Monkey," I said. "Take the Barbies to your room, and I'll be there in a minute to read."

"Toodle-oo," she said, then scooped up her dolls and all the hair she could and launched into a ballerina twirl out of the kitchen and across the den.

I picked up the sack and tip-toed back past the front room. The sound of Dad snoring made my head drop. I pulled the front door shut with a quiet click.

His truck was empty, the door wide open. Light from the cab spilled out onto the driveway.

"Real smooth, Ted," I said, and bumped it shut with my hip.

I looked up and down the street and didn't see him, so I walked through the side gate into the backyard. My bike was there, but I didn't see anything else.

Something banged around in the alley. I set the sack down, tiptoed around the mesquite trees, and quietly pulled myself up on the fence.

No Ted, but there were raccoons...about twenty of the filthy bandits. Fat ones, skinny ones, old ones, babies, all going nuts in our trash and ripping every shred of paper into the tiniest, most hard-to-clean-up pieces possible. More of them waddled down the alley.

"Aww, man," I groaned. "Thanks a lot, Ted." Leaving the lids off the trash cans was like ringing the dinner bell for every raccoon in the county. "Scram," I said.

Instead of running in fear of my power and command, they all laid their ears back, showed their crazy sharp teeth, and hissed.

"Whoa!" I jumped off the fence.

The door to the garage was still locked, which reminded me to close the side gate. Then I remembered that Preech and I accidentally broke the latch trying to wrestle a catapult he'd made out of the backyard, which exploded on the first launch attempt.

Finding some bricks lying by the house, I shoved them along the bottom to hold the gate shut.

I got in through the other back door, locked it, and made sure every door was secured. After a quick sweep through the house to make sure Ted hadn't somehow gotten inside, I went to Milly's room.

She was lying in bed, a huge pile of books on her bedside table. She grinned and yawned. "What took you so long?"

"Had to take care of some stuff. But don't worry, everything will be alright."

"'Kay."

"Scoot over." I stretched out beside her and grabbed the top book. "Cool, this one is about whales."

"What's that?" she asked, touching the picture on the front with water shooting out like a geyser.

I laughed. "You should like that. It's called a blowhole."

"That's not right. What's the hole that they stick cannons out of on pirate boats?"

"Port."

"Yes." She yawned again. "Then it's an air port, not a blowhole. Call the book maker; tell him he's wrong," she said, her voice fading from a sigh to a whisper.

And just like that, she was asleep.

I got up, slid a blanket over her, and tried to remember another one of Preech's "word for the day" from a couple of days earlier. Dissolve? No, no, the word was resolve. Yep, resolve. An unbreakable promise.

As I turned off her light and closed the door, I *resolved* to do everything I could to protect Milly and make sure she did not, and would not, have a worry in the world.

CHAPTER 6

The next morning, my alarm clock went off. I didn't know if I'd slept at all.

The night had been full of an endless stream of nightmares. I lay there and thought about everything from Ted's nostril-burning dragon breath to the sad picture of having separate Christmases with Mom and Dad. Were they actually getting a divorce? The word shot to the top of my list of all-time horrible words.

I jumped out of bed, threw on my shirt, lucky fishing hat, and jeans. When I turned on the light in my closet, I realized that one of my last pair of tennis shoes was probably floating around the pond, and the other was pinching the toes of a homicidal maniac.

Shoes belonged together, I thought, like hooks and swivels. Like Mom and Dad.

Remembering Dad had extras, I walked to their room. The bed was empty. A wave of panic hit me when I looked at the top of Mom's dresser. All of her jewelry, earrings, everything—gone.

Dad's shoes were about an inch too big, but they'd have to do.

A nervous energy boiled inside of me. I didn't know if it was a pull to get me to The Oracle's on time, or a push to create an escape from witnessing the awful sight of my parents' marriage, and our little family, crash and burn. *Why did Mom have to leave?*

I walked out of the house to an empty backyard. No bike, no Ted, nothing.

"Dangit," I said. The bricks next to the fence were scattered everywhere, and the gate was all busted up and hanging half off its hinges.

I ran to the fence, climbed up, and checked the alley.

"Double dangit." No bike or Ted, but there was an ocean of shredded napkins, bags, and food wrappers. It'd take me hours to clean everything up.

A powerful stench hung in the air. I didn't know if it was the trash getting ripe or if Ted's dragon breath had soaked into everything and forever polluted our alley. I walked back to the house, wondering if I should wake up Dad to give me a ride or if I could get to The Oracle's on time by running full speed the whole way.

Clumps of Barbie hair Milly had dropped on the den floor gave me an idea. I ran to the garage, and in it was her very small, very pink bike...complete with Barbie doll training wheels.

After doing a quick check inside to make sure Milly was still asleep (figuring she'd be less than positive about the idea), I grabbed the handlebars, rolled the bike out of the garage and over the bricks on the side of the house, hopped on, and took off.

At first, I tried to pedal normally, but my knees almost busted my chin, so I had to stand on them, cussing Ted with every stroke.

The Oracle's voice echoed in my head. "Boys, no matter where you're going, if you're on time, you're late." So I rode as fast as I could. There was a nagging feeling I was forgetting something. I realized my pocket was empty—no familiar thump of my lucky rock against my thigh.

My leg muscles burned, and the pink plastic tassels on the handlebars whipped my wrists as I turned off the asphalt and onto the crushed seashell road that led to The Oracle's farm.

The bushes next to the road exploded, and out of them flew a blur of golden fur.

"Gaah! You scared me half to death, boy."

Curi, The Oracle's golden retriever, jumped an inch away from the front tire, making me swerve and almost wipe out. "Hey, good dog! Who's a good dog?" I could barely make him out in the early dawn light, but I swear he frowned when he looked at the bike and then smiled when he recognized me. Curi took off towards the house, barking and dancing, his tail flying around so fast the whole back half of him wagged.

I snuck a peek at my watch as The Oracle's house came into sight. I had almost half a minute to spare.

Skidding to a stop next to the porch, I found Rudy and Preech bent over a table, staring at something in the dim porch light. Looking up at the same time, their eyes bugged out when they saw me and my ride. They stared at each other, then at me, and tried their best not to burst out laughing.

I smiled. "Go ahead."

They slapped each other on the back. Their hoots and giggles shattered the quiet morning air.

"I know, I know," I said. "Had a little problem with my bike."

"Bummer, dude. What's the issue?" Preech sniffed. "Sprockets? Gears? Crankset? Chain stay? Brakes? Brake cables? Spokes? Whatever problem you got, I can repair it pronto, amigo."

"Nope, umm." I had to think fast. "Let someone borrow it."

That was the first time I'd ever lied to my friends. Left a nasty taste in my mouth, like right after taking a gulp of spoiled milk.

"Let someone borrow your bike? Who?" Preech asked.

"Some guy, down the street, needed a ride to, uhh, find his cat or something."

A puzzled look grew on Preech's face. Butterflies exploded in my stomach. I pointed to the book they were looking at. "What's that?"

Preech lit up. "This is so awesome. Stories about all the countries in Europe and what you can visit and do."

He wiggled his fingers. "Did you know you could drive through, like, five different countries in the same distance it'd take you to drive across Texas?"

"Cool," I said, and hoped there wouldn't be any more bike questions.

"Oh, and another thing." He excitedly flipped through the pages. "If Uncle Oliver hasn't found his long-lost wife Marlena by this summer and he flies us over to help look, we might visit creations by a guy named Michelangelo. He made statues out of hunks of marble and stuff with a hammer and chisel."

Preech looked at me and grinned. "I bet he had a fantastically firm handshake, don't you?"

"Yeah," I said, but thought to myself that nobody had a handshake as firm as The Oracle. His was the best ever, like a friendly vice grip covered by a worn leather glove.

"Whoops," Rudy laughed as he squinted at the book. "Looks like he forgot that fella's pants and underwear."

Preech slid it away from him. "That is what they call art, you big, smelly dufus."

"Yoink!" Rudy snatched the book off of the table and held it over his head.

Preech reached as high as he could but was still a foot too short. "Gimme that."

Rudy shook his head. "Pfft, art."

He found a picture of a castle and traced his fingers along the words. "Now wait, here's an interesting story," he said.

"Once upon a time there was a soldier named Sir Preechalot, and the army he was with stormed the castle. Since the burning-hot oil they poured out could only make him look better, he was always the first up the ladder. He was almost to the top, but his skirt caught on the stones, and he fell into the moat where the gators chomped him to pieces."

"Ha, ha, whatever. Give it," said Preech.

Rudy smiled. "But wait, there's more! The attacking army was so happy Preechalot was finally gone that they laid down their bows and arrows, said thank you to the people they were attacking, and told them they'd tried to kill him in battle for years. Then everyone in the castle came out, and they drank and danced. But they were sad the gators died because he was so nasty. The end."

Rudy handed the book to Preech. He opened it to a dog-eared section and motioned me next to him for a better look. "I'm looking forward to Austria," Rudy said. "You know, with the kangaroos and those little gray bears with the great big ears."

Preech whipped his head towards me and crammed the back of his hand in his mouth to keep a laugh from escaping. I heard little bits of it slide around his knuckles.

I mouthed the words, "Is he thinking Australia?"

Preech nodded furiously and took a deep breath.

"Yep, Big Guy, you bet. The quicker we find Marlena, the quicker we go to Austria, Germany's next-door neighbor. And there are guys that make boomerangs from scratch; maybe you can make a trade with some stuff from Texas."

Rudy sighed. "So cool."

"What's weird," I said, "is that back in the war he was over there shooting at people and they were shooting back. What do you think he'll do if he recognizes one of them?"

Preech scratched his head. "What I've been wondering about is if they still have his leg, will they give it back so we can figure out a way to reattach it?"

Rudy shook his head. "Gee whiz, just when I think you can't get any weirder, you say something like that. Would they keep some random leg in a freezer for fifty years?"

"Would have actually been thirty-six or so years ago," Preech answered. "But, you know, shouldn't there be some kind of wartime respect for something like that? If I found a body part lying around, I'd preserve it and try to return it to its original owner."

"Whatever," Rudy said.

A voice boomed around us. "Mornin', soldiers."

We stood at attention and saluted.

"At ease," Oliver said, smiling as we all shook hands.

I glanced at his fingers and knuckles, wondering if punching Nazis in the face or working the ranch had put so many scars on them. You couldn't set a penny anywhere on his hand without covering one.

Instead of the overalls he normally wore, The Oracle was in full-blown camo. I pictured him in battle, chomping on a cigar with bullets flying everywhere, telling his troops how to wipe out the bad guys.

"We're in for a fine time today, troopers. Here are the marching orders." He reached back into the house and pulled out his chalkboard.

There were three things, in perfect handwriting, written across the top. The first one shot a jolt of panic through me.

1. Great news on diamond situation.

2. Hunting blind inspection and safe entry and exit.

3. Eradicate poison ivy explosion.

Oliver tapped the board with his cane. "Some excellent news. I got a letter from an old buddy of mine, Jimmy, who became a Naval hero by the way. He and his wife Lou will soon be coming through town as a stopover on a trip from California to South Carolina."

Preech's hand shot up. "Since they have gators over there, do they need someone to put tuna fish in his pockets and swim downcurrent to distract them? I nominate this bait ball." Preech pointed at Rudy. "He'd be awesome."

Oliver chuckled. "Well, I reckon we can ask. And maybe once you meet them, she'll tell you the great story on how she became a diamond expert."

He reached into his pocket and pulled out his lucky rock, nodding for us to do the same. "And we'll finally have clarity on what we've been carrying around all this time."

Preech and Rudy clinked theirs together, like doing a toast. Sparkles from the porch light danced across them.

They looked at me.

The Oracle smiled. "And yours, Private Kevin?"

"Oh, yes, sir," I said. "Mine is, uhh, in a super secure place...you know, for safe-keeping."

"Hmmm," he said, as he stroked his chin, leaned over, and offered his to me. "Why don't you put mine with yours? Sounds like a good plan."

The second his rock hit my palm, I got all queasy, like the wad of spoiled milk was coming back up.

Just great, I thought. One day with Ted, and I'd become a serial liar.

I crammed the shiny stone into my pocket as deep as it would go. "Will do, sir."

Oliver stared out into the cool, gray day. "First order of business will be safely executing the exercise of entering and exiting a hunting blind. Numerous accidents occur doing such things improperly, so we're going to practice until you three are experts. And we'll inspect them to make sure everything is in good shape."

Preech raised his hand. "Uncle Oliver, sir, some day, when you teach us how to hunt, would we have permission to shoot a zombie if we see one?"

The Oracle erupted with one of his loud, awesome belly laughs. It bounced and echoed up and down the porch.

"Absolutely. I give you full permission to shoot a bona-fide zombie if you catch one roaming around here. I'll double check with the game warden, but I'm pretty sure there's no limits or seasons on them."

I smiled at the thought of zombies coming out of the dirt at Old Man Perkins' place and terrorizing Ted. Did they eat diamonds? I hoped not.

"Private Preech, what say you run go grab the snake boots and hunting vests," Oliver said, then pulled up his camos, revealing his fake leg. "Did I ever tell y'all about getting nailed by a rattler in the back pasture?"

"No, sir," we said.

Oliver tapped two small, perfectly round holes in the tan-colored plastic, about knee-high. "Around this time of year, I was working the cattle." He held out two of his fingers like fangs. "I felt something hit me and found a two-footer hanging off my peg leg."

Rudy's eyes bugged out. "Whoa."

"'Whoa' is right. That devil was as surprised as me. Thinking I was surrounded by cow patties I realized there were rattlers everywhere. Just about every snake on the place had come out to sun."

"What'd you do?" Preech asked.

The Oracle made a pistol with his thumb and finger. "I annihilated 'em." He rubbed his belly. "And ate fried rattlesnake for a week straight."

Rudy grinned. "So cool."

"That being said, this year I'm upping the bounty to two dollars per rattle button for every rattle that y'all bring me."

"Excellent, I'll grab our stuff." Preech jumped off the porch, ran to the garage, and came back with boots and vests.

Oliver pointed to a big piece of plywood screwed to the side of his house. A map of the entire property was painted on it, complete with all four hunting blinds, and red arrows pointing out the direction of the firing lanes for each. There was a nail in the center of each blind.

"Troopers, we're going to split into two teams and double-time our mission today. As iron sharpens iron, I want y'all to monitor each other entering and exiting the blinds to point out anything that does not meet safety protocol. Since I can't climb into the ones in the tree tops, I'd also need a full report on the shape and condition of each. Roger that?"

"Roger," we said.

He picked up the spent .243 rifle shells with our names written on them and hung mine and Preech's on the screw that was in the blind farthest from the house. The shells were important because they would let the hunters know who was hunting where.

"Preech and Kevin, we're going to let you two recon this blind first, then we'll rendezvous in the center of the property, swap partners, and recon the other two."

The wooded part of the property kind of looked like a wagon wheel. The spokes were the paths that all met in the clearing in the middle, and there was one long path that circled the woods.

Preech saluted. "Sir, yes, sir."

"We'll all meet back at the one closest to the pond, and I will assess each of you for the final." He pushed his glasses up on his nose, squinted, and moved in for a closer look at the plywood map. "Speaking of the pond, appears somebody drew a couple hundred fish on it. That your handy work, Private Kevin?"

I blushed. "Yes, sir. Should we keep it like that?"

He nodded. "Affirmative. Gives it some character. Let's move out."

We slipped into snake boots and hunting vests. Oliver handed a walkie-talkie to Rudy, another to Preech, and they clipped them onto their belts.

There was a bit of a chill in the air, but not too cold. About the coolness of a catfish's skin that just came out of deep water.

Preech laughed. "Man, you gotta read that Europe book. A chapter about Ireland has a section of Irish blessings. Says things like, 'I hope your problems are as far apart as my grandmother's teeth.' Isn't that hilarious?"

"Yeah," I said, trying to sound interested, but thoughts of Ted buzzed around my head, making it hard to focus.

"And I'm going to learn the entire German language by the time we leave, so today's word for the day is 'Durchfall,' which means 'fall through,' and is their word for diarrhea. They are a very literal people!"

"Cool."

I sensed him looking at me. "You alright, amigo?"

My brain said, *Tell him about Ted, tell him about Ted,* but my mouth said, "Things have gotten real bad with my folks. Really, really bad."

"What's going on?"

"I don't know, came on tornado-fast. A week ago we were all happy, playing Monopoly. Milly was the angry banker, griping about every dollar she had to give us, and my folks were laughing and sitting so close they were practically in each other's laps."

"Well, if it happened quick, there should be some way to cure it quick." Preech skidded to a stop and snapped his fingers. "Flowers, dude. They've solved every single mom and dad problem ever...since caveman times, I think."

"Huh?"

"Look, my dad messes up *a lot.* Like constantly. But every time he does, he buys a big fancy bunch of them and gives them to Mom, and presto, everything's all good again."

"So grab some out of a ditch?"

"That strategy may be flawed, amigo. We need to leave the sunflowers in the dirt to attract doves for dove season, and if you accidentally pick a bluebonnet, I think you could get in trouble."

"Okay."

"Buy some from the flower shop and send them to your mom with a note that *says* they're from your dad. Then they'll be all 'Do you remember why we're fighting? Me neither! Love you so much!'"

He turned around and hugged himself. "Then the smooching starts." He rubbed his hands up and down his back.

Normally thinking of my parents kissing made me want to barf. But right then, I'd rather see that than a five-pound bass flop out of the pond on the end of my line.

"You think it'll work?"

"One hundred percent of the time, amigo. Have I ever steered you wrong? Everything is gonna be okay."

Then, just like that, one of the five-hundred-pound gorillas on my back got lighter, like it turned into a ten-pound monkey. I pictured Mom grabbing the phone, calling Dad at his office, and after hearing his apology, she'd jump in her station wagon and burn rubber all the way to him.

Preech was the absolute all-time smartest dude I'd ever met after The Oracle; I figured things like that ran in the family.

By the time we got to the blind, the sun was barely up. Preech clicked on the flashlight. "You know that The Oracle says Marines call these moonbeams. Isn't that cool?"

"Very cool. Hey, look, one of the pieces of wood covering the window is coming off. We need to tell him about that."

"Yep," Preech said as he handed me the flashlight and climbed the pieces of two-by-fours screwed to the tree that led up to the blind.

He got to the landing and pushed the door open. "All clear, except for a bunch of twigs and stuff. Did I do anything wrong getting up here?"

"Nope. You took your time and checked every board before putting any weight on it. If I could give you a grade higher than a hundred, I would."

"Awesome. Your turn."

I slipped the flashlight in my pocket, shoved it in hard to keep Oliver's lucky rock from escaping, and then climbed the ladder and stepped into the blind.

Preech took a seat on one of the two crates Oliver had us put in as chairs. I sat on the other. The crunch of sticks and leaves vibrated through the thick soles of my snake boots.

"Man, I guess a lot of stuff blew in through the busted window. Let's bring a broom and clean it out when we come back to fix things up."

"Sounds like a plan," Preech said, wrinkling his nose. "Does something smell funky in here to you?"

I took a long sniff. "Kinda does. Like a bear cave or something," I turned on the moonbeam and lit up the floor. "Huh, those sticks sorta look like bones."

"That's weird," Preech said. He unclipped the walkie-talkie from his belt, turned it on, and adjusted the knobs. "Alpha Leader, mission accomplished. Occupying target now." He grinned at me. "Private Kevin may have made the best blind entry maneuver in the history of mankind, giving him a perfect score. Over."

After a few seconds, Oliver's voice answered back. "Roger that. Everything ship-shape? Over."

"Yes, sir, affirmative. Mostly in good shape, but appears some minor repairs are in order. And a clean out due to window damage. Over."

Oliver's voice crackled back, but was drowned out by a blood-curdling screech. A blur of white and brown shot through the hole in the window.

CHAPTER 7

"No way, Ted, not today!" I yelled, but it wasn't him.

The biggest, baddest, angriest barn owl I'd ever seen swooped around us, his wings so long, they almost rubbed the wood on both sides of the blind.

Preech screamed as a freshly killed mouse splatted into his lap. He dove into the corner and hollered into the walkie-talkie. "May-day! May-day! Under attack! Abort mission!"

I lunged for the door, but the hovering beast beat me to it. One wing knocked off my lucky hat, and like a right hook, the other punched me square in the face. His evil beak and razor-sharp talons slashed the air, inches away from me.

I dove in the other direction, landed on top of Preech, and immediately discovered the stuff on the floor was bones, skulls, and piles of critter parts.

The owl swooped and dove around the inside of the blind, its wings creating a storm that stirred up fur and dust, making it impossible to see.

"Kill the sucker!" Preech yelled from underneath me.

"With what?"

There was a deafening bang and crack as the owl knocked the window covering completely off its hinges and escaped the blind.

I stayed on top of Preech for a few beats, then slowly opened my eyes and looked around the blind. Sunlight the color of our hunting vests poured in, and a haze of dust and floating fur particles swirled around us.

"I think he's gone," I said.

Oliver's voice crackled out of the walkie-talkie. "Status report. Situation? Over."

Preech's hand shook as he punched the button and whispered, "Attack is over. No casualties. An owl as big as a pterodactyl lives in this one. Over."

"Exercise caution getting out of there. Meet you at rendezvous point ASAP. Over."

Preech let go of the button. "Let's scram." We stood, I grabbed my lucky hat, and we shuffled out the door.

We got to the landing, and I pointed to the owl. It was on a branch about ten feet away, talons dug deep into the bark. Its dark eyes burned holes into mine.

"Nice and easy," Preech said as he descended the ladder. "No quick movements."

We got down and looked back at the owl.

"Creepy." Preech shivered. The owl stared at us, and then swiveled its head to look at the blind, and then back at us.

Preech brushed critter bits off of his pants and shirt. "Dude, that was nuts."

"Heck yeah. Thought we were gonna get our heads ripped off."

He smiled and cocked his head sideways. "Did you say something about 'Not today...Ted'?"

I thought fast. "Oh, that, uh, oh yeah. I told the devil bird to 'go away or you're dead,' or something like that. But I let him live since we weren't going to eat him."

He nodded. "Studly move."

We walked towards the center of the property. Preech motioned to a mound rising up in front of us. "Watch out for that. Almost tripped me a hundred times. The Oracle says it's barrels and stuff

44

moonshiners left here before he owned the property. Says we can dig everything up sometime if we want."

Moonshine, I thought. Why was that word important? It hung around in my head for a few seconds, and then evaporated (another one of Preech's "word for the day").

We met The Oracle and Rudy at the clearing in the center of the woods.

Oliver's face was creased with worry.

Rudy had a huge grin. "What happened? Did the little bird see the world's biggest worm and get all excited?"

"No," Preech said. "It was an all-out assault. We're lucky to be alive." He pointed at me, his finger still shaking a bit. "And my main man Kevin here acted as a human shield to protect me. Is there a commendation or something for that, Uncle Oliver?"

"Duly noted." The Oracle lifted his cane to the blood stain on Preech's pants. "Y'all sure you're okay? You injured?"

"No, sir. I believe it's from the breakfast mouse he dropped on me." Preech tried to scratch the crimson spot off with his fingernail.

Rudy snickered.

"Well," Oliver said, "I reckon I'd drop my groceries too if I walked into my house and two giant owls were sitting at my dinner table."

Rudy put his arm around my shoulders. "Glad you're okay, Kev." He looked at Preech. "And barn owls have just become one of my favorite animals. I think they're cool."

Preech frowned. "I think they're psycho."

"Okay, troops, let's have Rudy and Kevin recon the third blind, and Private Preech and I'll do the other. Then we'll meet back at the house."

Preech raised his hand. "And what do we do with the owl blind? Burn the place down? That creature is a menace."

"Negative," Oliver said. "We're going to build him a better habitat in the area, bait it with some fresh catch to lure him in, and see if he'll relocate on his own."

"Are you sure about that, sir?" Preech asked. "The hideous beast may want human blood from now on."

Oliver chuckled. "I want to keep him around to assist in keeping the mice and other small critter populations in check. I've heard they even eat bats."

Rudy nodded. Preech shook his head.

Rudy and I started down the path to the other blind. The flashlight slipped out of my pocket, bounced off of my knee, and skidded down the path.

I picked it up and wiped off the dirt. "Did you know Marines call these 'moonbeams'?"

"Cool," Rudy said. "You think it's because the beam of light is the same color the moon shines?"

There was that word again, moonshine. And—BAM! —it hit me: part of an answer to the Ted problem.

Since I was lying to the rest of the world, why not lie to Ted?

A warm, fuzzy feeling glowed inside me as a plan "materialized" (another one of Preech's "word for the day") in my head. Tell Ted the jeweler got back in town, said the lucky rocks were worthless sea glass, swap him food, aspirin, and a bottle of moonshine, which had to be way better than whiskey, for my lucky rock. But what about the problem with the letter? I'd figure something out by the time I got to Old Man Perkins' place. I was on a roll!

We reached the other blind which wasn't as high as the first one. I counted five two-by-four ladder rungs instead of nine, but plenty high to have a winged creature of death living in it.

"Yo, bud," I said, "let's walk around and look for any holes that a giant face-ripping critter could use."

Rudy nodded. "Good thinking."

I picked up a rock and chunked it at the blind. "Demons out!"

Rudy grabbed a long branch off the ground and beat the wooden sides.

We waited, listened, and heard nothing.

"Alright," Rudy said, "I'm going in." He climbed up, opened the door, and the blind swallowed him.

Two seconds later, he screamed. "Aaah! Stop! Stop it!"

CHAPTER 8

"Coming, buddy!" I grabbed the branch he'd left on the ground.

His head poked out of the blind, and he smiled. "Is that how the twerp sounded when the itty-bitty bird flew in?"

I laughed, more relieved than entertained. "Yeah, kind of. It was crazy."

He climbed down, and we met up with Preech and The Oracle.

"Okay, troopers," Oliver said. "A couple more marching orders to tend to today. Private Preech, do you recall the ivy experiment you initiated in my greenhouse a few months back?"

Preech's eyes lit up. "My poison-ivy/Johnson-grass/bamboo hybrid plants? Did they take off?"

"Affirmative. Exceptionally well. Looks like Vietnam in there. I'm going to need you three to mitigate the situation. After that, we'll grab some grub."

We got back to the house. Preech nodded his head sideways towards his bike, signaling me to come with him. Once we were out of earshot, he whispered, "Hey, how about you say you gotta go do something, which we both know you do, and me and Meathead can clean things up. Got money for flowers?"

I felt my pockets. "Nope."

"No problem." He whipped out his wallet and gave me all the cash he had: two five-dollar bills. He took off his belt, flipped it over, and to my surprise there was a tiny zipper that ran down the middle. He unzipped it, slid out two more fives, and handed them to me.

Preech snapped his fingers and dug into the mountain of things hanging on his bike. He extracted (another of his "word for the day") his pocket protector, a soft plastic pouch about as big as a chalkboard eraser, and he emptied out the pens, pencils, and protractors and handed them to me. He cut his eyes at Rudy, who was on the porch looking at the Europe book with The Oracle. "There's no doubt who filled this half-full with glue the other day, but when I cleaned it out, I discovered the inside lining separates from the outside lining for a perfect hidey-hole." He reached in, plucked out a ten-dollar bill, and handed it to me.

I rubbed the money between my fingers. "Dude, this is a ton of cash. I don't think I have enough at home to pay you back."

"No sweat, amigo, I know I can count on you. Now jump on that sweet ride and go make your world alright again. When you're done, we'll take the raft on its first voyage and catch some big ones."

We high-fived. I ran to Milly's bike and waved to Oliver and Rudy. "Thank you for today, sir. I have to head home to take care of some stuff."

He saluted me. "Good time today, private. See you soon."

I saluted him back. "Sir, yes sir."

Rolling down the driveway, Oliver's voice boomed around me. "Make sure you two put on long-sleeve work shirts and gloves to clean out the poison ivy. We may need to burn them afterwards."

I wondered if I should hunt down the flowers or moonshine first. The training wheels squeaked when they hit the asphalt. "Moonshine, of course, so the flowers will be fresher," I whispered. "Excellent! I'm on fire!" The toy bike and I headed to see Mr. Swafford, the Willy Wonka of fish bait and tackle.

CHAPTER 9

I rode up Mr. Swafford's driveway, parked Milly's bike, and smiled when I caught a whiff of the catfish dough bait curing in tubs and sealed buckets on the front porch. The sour twang of cheese and blood baits grew stronger as I got closer, which made me gag a little and grin bigger all at the same time.

I eased the front door open. "Hello, Mr. Swafford, you here?"

"That you, Kevin? Sure am, in the kitchen. C'mon back."

His voice carried around the mounds of fishing tackle and bathtubs full of dirt and worms and above the whirr of aerators keeping minnows alive in the metal tanks set along the walls. I worked my way to the kitchen, picturing *exactly* what my house would look like someday. I'd like never having to clean up a thing.

Mr. Swafford was bent over the sink, full of crappie.

I whistled. "Good haul, sir. Where'd you catch them?"

He smiled and pointed his knife at the pile of gleaming fillets on the counter. "Helped a friend of mine take some out of his pond. They're bedding in skinny water right now, about a foot or two deep. Need hooks? Minnows?"

My mouth watered as I stared at the slabs, picturing Oliver pulling golden fried fish nuggets out of steaming hot grease covered with beer batter, and then pouring his super-secret melted salt and pepper butter sauce on top. "I wish. Got a bunch of other stuff I gotta do today." Right when I was about to ask him for the moonshine, my mouth stopped working. *Snap out of it!* said the voice in my head. *He's the nicest guy in town, and we need some for the plan to work. Do not chicken out.* I rubbed the sweat off my palms onto my pants. "Well, umm, Mr. Swafford sir, I'm actually looking for something else."

He laid down his fillet knife and wiped his hands with a rag. "Sure. New pole? Bait bucket?"

"Moonshine?" I asked. My whole body winced.

His eyebrows rose. "What makes you think I got something like that around here? And if I did, what in the world would you need it for?"

I didn't have an answer for that. There was no way I could tell him about the time Preech and I snooped around the back of his property where we found all the big copper pots that looked like dead robots. I thought fast. "Oh, no, not to drink or anything. I figured you may have something like that I could use for, uhh, for school stuff?"

He crossed his arms, leaned back against the counter, and scowled. "So, your school needs some for what?"

Sweat trickled down my spine. I tried to look him in the eye, but couldn't. "Umm, no sir, I just, uh, actually need something like that for an experiment...yeah, for an experiment they gave us over spring break. To bring things back for, you know, umm, fuel sources and stuff." I mentally kicked myself for such a pathetic answer.

He shook his head, picked up his knife, and pulled a crappie out of the sink. "Can't help you there, young man."

Do it for Milly, I thought. *You promised to protect her. Having some will help get the lucky rock back. Then we'll figure out the other stuff.* I crossed my heart. "Swear I wouldn't drink a drop, sir. I hope it would really help me earn a good grade. And I'll hopefully be a successful businessman like yourself someday."

He laughed, set his knife down, bent over, and stared at me so hard it made the back of my brain itch.

"Well, to be honest, I do make some home-grown hooch to sip on cold fishing nights. Moonshine is an ugly word, so it's more like human anti-freeze if you hear what I'm sayin'. But I'd be less than comfortable giving you any, so please understand where I'm coming from when I say I can't help you." He turned back to the fish.

I twisted the other way, pulled out the cash, and thought about giving him one of the five-dollar bills. The voice in my head said *Go big, or go home,* so I snagged the ten and crammed the rest back in my pocket. The money crinkled in the quiet room as I smoothed it out on the counter. "Will this help?"

He blinked at the money, then at me, and then at the ten-spot again. "So, this'll be for education purposes? Absolutely no way you're gonna drink a drop?"

I grinned and shook my head. "No way, sir. Not a chance."

"Well, I have something that may work." Mr. Swafford and the cash disappeared out the back door. He returned with a bottle of clear liquid. I counted eight rubber bands that secured an aluminum foil cap on top.

"Now, this batch turned out bad for some reason. Took a sip the other day and couldn't see right for two days straight."

"Okay," I said.

"I think the squirrels or possums got in and used it for a toilet or something, so this stuff ain't exactly fit for human consumption anyway, if you get my drift."

I nodded.

"I was going to use some to start a brush fire, but if it can further your education, I figure that'd be a better use. One more time, no chance of this touching your lips, right?"

I raised my hand. "Sir, I'd put my hand on every Bible you have and promise—no, not promise—resolve, that me or my friends will not drink a drop." Man did it feel good to tell the truth again.

"Resolve? That's a fancy word. Alright then, these fish won't clean themselves, so you go on and be safe."

"Yes sir, will do. Thank you again."

Mr. Swafford smiled. "No problem." He reached into his shirt pocket, pulled the money out, and handed it back to me. "Tell you what. I don't feel right taking this, so what say you come help me out with some things around here to work it off. Maybe part-time at first, then see where things go."

He pushed the cash into my palm. "Me? Work for you? Here? That would be awesome!"

"It's a deal." We shook on it. "Have your folks give me a call to go over details to make sure they're okay with the situation."

I nodded, and walked towards the front door, being extra careful not to trip and accidentally spill any, or even worse, drop it and cause a weird chemical reaction at my brand-new workplace. "Will do. Thank you again so much, for everything." Easing down the front steps, I realized my luck had returned. It was *back*, baby. And with luck, my parents wouldn't split up, my lucky rock would be mine again, I'd figure out a way to dodge a jail sentence, and maybe even hook a huge fish.

Hello, luck, I thought. *Missed you, old friend.* And the best thing? I'd cracked into the bait business!

I wrapped the human anti-freeze like a baby in an old towel I found in the front yard, set it in the basket on the front of Milly's bike, and headed for the flower shop.

Focusing hard to dodge the potholes, as I rolled into town, I heard someone say, "You, hold it right there."

Officer Duncan and Officer Shipley, the policemen that had busted Ted, stepped off the curb and walked into the street towards me.

Seeing them made sweat pour out of every sweat hole in my body.

53

"Where are your partners in crime?" Officer Shipley smiled and pulled his nightstick out and lightly tapped the bell on Milly's bike.

"Crime, what crime?" I asked, betrayed by my voice that squeaked like a hinge on a jailhouse door. *Well*, said the voice in my head, *there's the fact you have illegal hooch, and you're too young to have legal or illegal hooch, and you're aiding a known felon. Oh, and there's the little problem of—Shut up*, I told the voice.

Officer Duncan snickered. "Sure is a pretty little ride you got there. Think you'll be able to take the training wheels off before you start shaving?"

Be cool, said the voice in my head, obviously unable to take an order. *Remember what The Oracle says: every time you see a member of the law or military, shake their hand, look them in the eye, and thank them for what they do.*

I offered my hand to shake theirs. "Ha, ha, no sirs, having some problems with my bike. Had to borrow my sister's."

Officer Shipley and I shook, and he asked, "Haven't seen you since that little dust up in the Flats. Y'all haven't thought about doing some fool thing like heading out there again, have you?"

I sucked in a breath and shook my head. "No, sir." I hoped I'd never have to get close to that horrible, scary place again.

Officer Duncan smiled. "Good to hear. Hey, we've had a sudden rash of petty thefts and other shenanigans lately."

"Oh?"

"Nothing major, some things coming up missing around town. You seen or heard anything suspicious?" He nodded towards the war memorial in the middle of the town square. Sawhorses surrounded the area, and an officer I didn't recognize was studying the scene with a magnifying glass. "The darnedest thing is somebody stole the new time capsule they'd set in there yesterday. Dug it out before the concrete totally hardened." Officer Duncan took off his police hat and scratched his head. "Wasn't much of worth inside. Mostly books and records and newspapers and such, but the city council sure is spun up about things."

I vaguely remembered Mr. Deleon, our social studies teacher, geeking out about the time capsule a few weeks earlier. But I believe I was catching a thousand-pound marlin in my head at the time, and didn't absorb (one of Preech's "word for the day") all the details.

"You think the escaped convicts committed the crime?" I asked, immediately scared to hear the answer.

"Nope, no way," he said. "We're confident both of the missing inmates are dead. Superman himself couldn't have survived that fall."

"Really?"

He nodded. "The feds figure they got mashed up good, so they're setting nets further down river to retrieve whatever pieces they can."

Officer Shipley's nightstick slid from Milly's bell to the moonshine wrapped in the towel. "What you got there?"

I had to think super-duper fast, and just like that, WHAM! One of Preech's weird experiments on human body function hit me.

"You're more than welcome to check it out, but, ummm, took me a week to fill up so please don't spill any. Had to drink like eight gallons of tea."

His nightstick jerked away from it. "What?"

"I have some more at home. One bottle is from a whole week of eating asparagus. Same color, but definitely different aroma. If you know what I mean."

Almost tripping over each other, they stepped backwards onto the sidewalk. The smiles on their faces were gone, replaced with something I couldn't quite decipher. Disgust? Horror, maybe?

"You got issues, son," Officer Shipley said as he wiped his hand and nightstick off on his pants.

I smiled the biggest smile I could. "Oh, and by the way, thank you both for all—"

"Beat it, kid," Officer Duncan said.

"Oookay." I forced the tiny pedals to do their job. Thanks to Ted, I figured I'd probably just been put on some kind of police "Weirdo Watch List."

In front of me, a guy that worked at Grease Monkeys walked onto the sidewalk to spark up a stinky cigar, so I checked for traffic, rode across the street, went down half a block, and rode back across to Flower Power. I parked Milly's bike out front.

Opening the door, a wall of smell from a million different flowers filled my nose, so thick I could almost chew it. The lady behind the counter rubbed her hands on her apron. "Hello, honey."

"Hello, ma'am. I need to buy some flowers, please. A whole bunch of them."

"Sure thing. What kind?"

I scratched my chin and thought. What were they called? It was a flower with the same name of a lady I knew.

Was it Rose, the cool cafeteria lady that always slid me an extra patty on hamburger day? No. Was it Iris, the secretary at Dad's architect office that gave me a handful of peppermints every time I walked by her desk? Nope.

Pride filled my chest when I finally remembered, just like Rudy's mom's name: Daisy.

I spread the cash out on the counter. "How many daisies will this buy?"

Her eyes lit up. "Pretty much every single one I've got, plus some gorgeous filler flowers. How do you want them?"

"In a nice vase, and in one of those boxes y'all have if that wouldn't be too much trouble. Gotta get them there in one piece."

She smiled and nodded. "Who should I make the card and box out to?"

"Make it out to 'Mom.' No wait, to 'Connie' would be better."

"Okay," she said.

I thought for a second. If it was going to work, I'd have to go all out. "Oh, no wait." I leaned in and whispered, "How about make it out to 'Snuggle Bunny.'"

Much, much too loudly, she repeated, "Snuggle Bunny?"

My cheeks burned.

"Hmm, sounds like someone's in trouble."

"Not for long, I hope."

"Who should I say they're from?" she asked.

My cheeks got hotter. I picked up a pen and wrote "Sugar Whomper" on a piece of paper, slid it to her, and said, "Think that's how you spell it. I have no idea what that means."

She grinned. "In all my years, I've seen flowers cover a multitude of sins. Think I've got some that'll do the trick." Buzzing around the shop, it only took her a few minutes to pull together the prettiest pile of flowers I'd ever seen. She put the vase in the box, signed it, and taped it shut. "There you go. Every daisy I got, plus some lovely extras to give you your money's worth. The little white ones are called Angel's Breath, my favorite."

I thanked her and walked out of the store. "Angel's Breath," I said. "Good to hear. Gonna need all the help I can get." The box fit snugly in the basket next to the human anti-freeze, securing each other for the ride.

I breezed down the street, ringing Milly's bell, not caring at all who saw me. The sappy song "Top of the World" by the Carpenters popped into my head, and I pictured how Mom and Dad would play the record and dance and sing as they listened to it over and over. *Oh yes, they'll be dancing and singing again, possibly tonight,* I thought, and the vision made me pedal even harder.

When I turned onto our street, I felt delighted (one of Preech's "word for the day") to see Mom's car in the driveway, which proved my luck was back. I wouldn't have to figure out how to deliver the flowers all the way across town to Deedee's.

I parked Milly's bike on the side of the house, tapped Ted's new bundle of joy, and whispered, "Stay." Crouching under the windows, I snuck to the front door and carefully set the flowers on the porch.

I swung the door open. "Hey, Mom, think there's something here for you!"

"In here," she said.

I walked into the front room, and my heart dropped. She was surrounded by boxes, putting what seemed like everything we had into them. "What was that, Kevin?"

"A package came for you."

"A package? For me?"

She walked to the door. I half-ran, half-skipped to the kitchen window, trying to get there in time to see her face when she opened the one thing that would make everything better.

I got to the window, about to poke my head out, and the flowers flew by about a hundred miles an hour. The vase exploded against the brick wall at the end of the porch, inches away from my face.

CHAPTER 10

As the front door slammed shut, she yelled, "Trying to kill me?"

"Daaaannggg," I said, remembering what it was about Mom and daisies. At my uncle's wedding a few years earlier, I was sitting in my scratchy Sunday shirt in the boiling summer heat. Mom was halfway down the aisle before she passed out, tripped one of the other bridesmaids, and squashed the daisies she was carrying.

A doctor there said she was "deathly allergic" to them, so instead of delicious wedding cake, all I got to eat that day was ice chips in the emergency room while they fixed her up. I really knew I'd messed up when, through the wall, I could hear her do that thing where she was talking to herself and laughing at the same time.

I tip-toed back to the front room and peeked around the door. Her head hadn't swollen up like a watermelon, but man, she was mad. She ripped tape off the roll, slammed it on a box, slung it out of the way, and reached for another one. She stopped and glared at me. "Yes, Kevin?"

"Umm, you okay?"

"No. I am not. Sometimes your father has a very inappropriate sense of humor. We're enduring a very trying time right now, and stunts like that definitely do *not* help."

She said the word "father" like she was spitting out poison. The voice in my head went nuts, screaming louder than ever. *Ask her why they don't go to a therapist or pastor to save everything! Ask her what you did and what you can do to fix it! Tell her you sent the bonehead killer flowers!*

Tell her she can't leave; there's no way Dad can figure out the washing machine! The cutter on that big roll of tape looks sharp; careful what you say! I tried to make words, but nothing came out, like every piece of tape in the world was wrapped around my head, clamping my teeth together.

She picked up a box and pushed past me towards the front door. "If you've got nothing to say, Milly and I have to leave. Please go tell her."

I kicked myself as I walked to my room to grab my money. Mom and Dad needed to get fixed, but I felt like I'd thrown a gas can into a fire that was way, way out of control.

I picked up the Bible on my dresser. Nothing was there. I stomped to Milly's room.

She was hunched over her desk. A bottle of glue lay on its side, a white puddle the size of a dinner plate pooled around it. Her face was scrunched together, the tiny pink tip of her tongue poking out of the side of her mouth.

"Hey, did you take my cash?"

She looked up. Clumps of brown and blonde hair stuck to her face, her hands, the magnifying glass she was holding, and the desk. A Barbie doll was laid out like a patient on an operating table.

"Pffft," she said. A long piece of yellow plastic hair shot out of her mouth. "Yep. Gave the money to my friend." She held up her little finger. "He pinkie promised to give it back, plus more."

"Friend?" I pointed under the bed. "You mean Leo, the Leprechaun Hippo? Tell him I need it. I owe Preech."

She turned back, focusing on her mission. "Not that one, silly. Pfft. I got a new friend."

I opened the closet door. "Where does he live, in here?"

"Nope, not the clothes hole. You're getting warmer."

"In one of your drawers?"

60

"Nope, he came to my window and wears the funniest outfits." And in a super-deep voice, Milly said, "He's huge and has the reddest hair ever." She turned in her chair and pointed to her nose. "He's very grumpy, and his booger holes are definitely *not* clean, but his shiny bracelet has a hole for a key. So pretty!"

I walked to the window and looked down at two footprints in the dirt. A shiver ripped through me that almost lifted me off the carpet.

One footprint had a shoe; the other one didn't.

I slammed her window shut, locked it, and tried to talk normally, but instead yelled, "Listen, you can't—"

Mom's voice shot down the hall. "Milly, I'm leaving in ten seconds. Very long walk to Deedee's."

Milly's eyes bugged out. "Gotta go." She jumped up, grabbed a pillow off her bed, and scraped the gooey mess of dolls, hair, and glue into the pillowcase. "Hey, call the police. Somebody swiped my bike!"

"It was me."

She skidded to a stop and whirled around so fast her ponytail shot straight up in the air. "What? Why?"

"Long story."

Mom's car horn blared.

Milly took off. "My new friend's bike looks like yours. Ask him where he got his if you need a new one. And put mine back."

I followed her outside and watched them tear out of the driveway, feeling as hollowed out and empty as the crumpled-up box with "To My Snuggle Bunny" written across the front. Did she say red hair? I was sure Ted's was black. Maybe she meant the ugly red volcano of grossness rising out his beluga whale-like head. The image of him getting that close to her twisted my stomach into knots.

I got rolling on Milly's bike and thought through what I had to do: get my lucky rock back, figure out the Ted situation, and then fix Mom and Dad.

As Old Man Perkins' house came into view, fear crawled up my spine like a tarantula.

The busted windows were like eyes, and the hole where the front door had been looked like a mouth caught mid-scream.

CHAPTER 11

I rolled into a clump of trees by the road and stared through the leaves to see what was creeping around the place. Ghosts? Demons? Goblins? At least vampires and werewolves only came out at night. Or did they?

Peeling the towel away from the bottle, a familiar scent filled the air. A few drops had seeped around the foil lid and raced down the slick glass. I took a closer sniff. It smelled exactly like the weird chemicals Mom used to take off her nail polish.

"Nasty...How can people actually drink this stuff?" I moved my hand so the liquid wouldn't touch me, wondering if it'd burn a hole in my skin or leave some kind of weird tattoo.

Okay, I thought, *try to remember everything The Oracle taught us about walkabout hunting so I can sneak up on the place and see them before they see me. And first sight of anything that thirsts for boy blood or brains, run back to the bike and burn rubber.*

Every part of me screamed to leave, but my legs slowly took me towards the house. Something crunched and cracked under my shoe, breaking the number one rule of being quiet while on the hunt. "Please don't be zombie fingers. Please don't be zombie fingers," I repeated.

I started breathing again when I realized it was only a pile of sticks. The voice in my head said, *Get your stuff together, man. We've got a mission to accomplish.*

First thing, be as silent as possible. Next, check windage. I studied the trees. Leaves were blowing in my direction. Not much, but enough to push my scent away and prove I was downwind. Good.

I could almost feel The Oracle next to me, telling me what to do, like my very own countrified Obi-Wan Kenobi. I stuck to the shadows, walked sideways to shrink my profile, and stopped every few steps to look with my eyes instead of my whole head to minimize movement.

Getting close to the house, I remembered him saying dirt tells the story of everything that lives and eats around an area. I saw tracks everywhere. Some looked like those of either a very fat or very pregnant opossum, deer tracks from either a fawn or tiny doe, and something that resembled a swirl.

Did ghosts make swirls when they came and went from the afterlife? I hoped not.

There were also tons of human footprints—some with shoes, some without—and bicycle tire tracks. There was something odd about the prints, though, but there was so much zipping around my head, I couldn't focus on what it was.

A long, painful moan floated out of the house of horror. I turned on my heels, ready to shatter the world record for sprinting back a hundred yards to the bike, and somebody started...crying? It got louder. Hard crying, like four quick breaths in and a loud slobbery sob back out.

I tip-toed to a shattered window on the side of the house surrounded by bruise-colored wood. Peeking through, I saw Ted sitting cross-legged on the floor. He was facing away from me, holding something familiar in his hand. It was the photo that usually sat on top of Rudy's TV, the one of him and his mom in her workout shirt that said, "Sweat is fat crying."

A bolt of terror shot through me when I realized that the maniac had been *inside* Rudy's home.

"Ted?"

He threw the picture, jumped to his feet, and spun around. "Dangit, punk. Don't ever do that. You could give someone a heart attack." Ted grimaced as he limped and staggered towards the window, like he was wearing sandpaper underwear, barely missing a massive crater in the floor.

There were holes in the walls, floors, ceiling, everywhere. I wondered if ghosts had fired cannons at each other. The house was so creaky and unstable, I figured a butterfly burp would make the shack crash into a heap of toothpicks.

To my surprise (and relief), human bones and teeth weren't scattered everywhere, but the air had a weird, old smell, like rotten dirt.

Ted inched closer. The bump on his head had shrunk from softball-sized to tennis-ball-sized. Sunlight streamed in from holes in the roof, highlighting all of the lump's hideous grossness. It was like a bulging wad of day-old roadkill, complete with two flies on the top, wondering what to do with it.

Ted blew his nose in his hand, wiped it on the wall, and limped the last few steps. He leaned into the center of the jagged shards of broken glass that circled the window like shattered teeth. "What?"

His dragon breath was still cranked up to full-on nasty. A wave of it pushed me back a step, making vomit tickle the back of my throat.

His scratch-covered arm bumped the windowsill. He winced and pulled back.

I stared at the oozing gashes. "Whoa, are those from the accident, sir?"

"Can't recollect much, but I do recall getting all tore up by a pack of wild animals in your alley." He dragged out the words "tore up" like it hurt to say them.

I made a mental note to buy a pack of hot dogs to feed my new friends, the raccoons. Without the wrapper, of course.

Ted started to weave. His knee buckled, and he grabbed the wall to keep from falling over. The chain on his handcuff went into a clicking frenzy.

"Ted, sir, should I try to find you a doctor or something?"

Ignoring me, he said, "What's today?"

"Monday."

"You ain't got school no more, do you?"

"We're on spring break, sir."

"Never seen a boy grow taller but his muscles get smaller like yours did. Figured your brain was shrinkin', too, and you got so stupid you couldn't go anymore." He stared at the bottle. "Whatcha got there?"

"You said to bring you some whiskey to get my lucky rock back, right? Umm, here you go, sir. We found out they're just, uhh, worthless pieces of sea glass." I faked the biggest and cheesiest grin I could.

He scowled back and patted his pants pockets, then his breast pocket, and grunted as he pulled it out.

Sunlight ricocheted off my little friend, smiling to see me again.

His finger jabbed at the human anti-freeze. "Gimme that first."

I eased the bottle to him, trying to keep from slicing my arms on the razor-sharp glass.

He ripped off the foil lid, took a long sniff, and nodded. He reached through the window, holding my lucky rocks by his fingertips. I opened my palm to catch it, trying my hardest *not* to remember if that was the same hand he'd used to blow his nose.

Ted paused. I looked up to see him staring directly into my eyes...a burning stare; I swear it roasted part of my brain.

"On second thought, I'm gonna get me another opinion to see if this is real. My friend that stays on the river knows a lot. Especially how to keep his mouth shut."

"Scary Larry?" I asked, thinking about the weird guy that lived in an old broken-down school bus and the main reason why we never fished that stretch of water.

"His name is Lawrence, you worthless punk." Ted's fingers sucked up my lucky rock and balled into a fist around it. "He's one of the smartest fellas in town; just chooses to live different."

"Okay, sir, understood."

His eyes turned to slits. "Know what? You should really get the whole story before you go around all half-cocked, shooting your mouth off like you know everything." He tapped a shard lying on the windowsill. The glass screamed as he ran my lucky rock down its center, splitting the glass clean in two.

Ted smirked. "Diamonds cut glass; sea glass don't. This is mine."

Panic surged through me. "But you said we'd trade. You, umm, promised. Remember?"

"Well, boo-hoo. Go cry to someone else. Stuff happens." He sighed. "But, even though you ain't worth spit, you're lucky Ted's a man of his word. I'll trade you something."

Ted turned and limped back through the room, shuffling around the holes and setting the moonshine down by the picture as he passed by.

I stepped closer.

There were more weeds growing inside than out. Broken pieces of furniture, torn up magazines, and shattered bottles littered the floor. I noticed something in the corner. There wasn't a grimy gray fuzz covering it like everything else, so I figured it was new. There was an odd-shaped metal box, but too far away to see what was inside. Next to the box was a radio.

Officer Duncan's words about things coming up missing drifted into my head.

Ted turned and saw me looking at it. "I heard on the squawk box earlier the pinhead cops think I'm fish food, twenty miles downriver."

He wagged his finger and waved my lucky rock around the room. "If I see anyone or anything but you, I guarantee I got a thousand ways to make this disappear."

I blinked. The hope of getting my stone back bled out of me like air out of a balloon.

"And," he continued, "Rudy told me everyone in your little gang of maggots got one. Once I heal up, I may pay a visit to claim their rocks as my own. Including that old, crusty one-legged dude. What do ya think about that?"

I tried to answer, but it felt like my throat had squeezed shut.

"Got manure in your ears, boy? You hear what I'm sayin'?"

I nodded. "Yes, sir. Loud and clear, sir."

"Maybe you ain't as dumb as you look." Ted staggered to the metal box, reached in, and pulled out...a book. He got about halfway to the window, stopped, and chunked it. The hardback sailed right through the hole in the glass.

I caught the twirling blur, inches away from my face. "Gee, thanks, sir." I tucked the book into my armpit. "Sooo, about my bike?"

He shook his head. "I ain't got that, due to the pack of critters that ripped me up and all."

I glanced down at the tire tracks in the dirt. "I really need my ride back. Please?"

"Did you find out why Rudy railroaded me with that fake letter? Is he gonna do the right thing and fess up?"

An image of me, Preech, and Rudy wearing prison black-and-whites busting big rocks into smaller rocks flashed through my mind. "Yes, umm, well that I'm working on. No news yet, working on things, sir."

"Your bad habit of lettin' me down is gettin' worse, punk."

"Understood, sir, will figure that out for you."

"Yoww!" Ted collapsed next to the picture and grabbed his bare foot. I hoped a goblin had jumped up and bit him. He pulled two stickers off his heel, flicked them down a hole, and hooked a thumb over his shoulder. "Maybe he's got it."

"He? Who?"

By taking a couple of steps to the right, then a couple to the left, I could see every square inch of the house through the Swiss cheese walls. *Hoo boy,* I thought. *He's seeing things. Did the head blow scramble his brains?*

"Been thinkin', since they figure me a ghost, it'd be best if I laid some miles between me and here for a time, let you get things straightened out for Ted. Go fetch me some cash, clothes, and grub."

"Cash? You got all mine."

He stood up and slid his hands into his pockets. His face twisted with confusion. "I do?"

His fingers appeared through the holes in his pants, obvious that the bottoms of the pockets were long gone. Great.

He picked up the picture, and his face changed. It went kind of soft, almost kid-like. Rubbing the image of Daisy like a baby rabbit, he said, "I do recollect going by my house to pick up my clothes. Couldn't find any." His chin trembled. "You reckon she sent them to the cleaners or somethin'? To make me happy when I got back?"

I remembered Rudy telling me that the night the divorce was final, he and his mom made a bonfire out of Ted's clothes so tall the flames burned higher than the roof of his house.

"Oh yeah, probably so," I lied.

He blinked and nodded. Then, just like that, Angry Ted was back. "Get outta here. You're smellin' up the place."

"Yes, sir," I said. I walked back to Milly's bike, wrapped the book in the towel, and headed home.

Dad's truck was in the driveway. I parked the tiny bike by the side of the house, trying to figure out how everything had gotten so crazy.

A couple of days earlier my biggest problem was wondering if Dad would let me borrow his golf shoes with the shiny spikes to wear on the raft, so there'd be something to bite into the wood and keep a gargantuan fish from pulling me into the water.

I turned the corner by the garage, and almost ran into him. His drill was in one hand, and his other arm was in a sling.

CHAPTER 12

"Oh, no, Dad. What happened?"

"For some cockamamie reason, your mother locked the garage door. Went to open it and almost ripped my arm out of its socket." He set the drill on a pile of tools in the back of his truck, climbed in, and cranked the engine.

The voice in my head went nuts. *Tell him you locked the door! And it was you who sent the daisies of death so he doesn't get hammered for it! Where's he going with his stuff? Is he moving out, too? You and Milly won't survive; the only thing close to food she can make is mud pies. Ask him what you did. Say something!*

"Dad!" I yelled over the revving motor.

He poked his head out of the window and cupped his hand behind his ear.

My voice cracked. "I'm, umm, sorry."

He nodded. "We all are, buddy. Gotta go." He backed out of the driveway and took off.

Why'd you say that? asked the voice in my head. "Shut up," I said, and then got back on Milly's ride and rode towards The Oracle's.

Fishing—just thinking about something so cool calmed me down a bit. A quick trip to the pond, put a hook in the water, clear my head, help me start thinking straight again. It'd be good medicine, like they said on the westerns I watched with my dad. Or used to.

Something in the ditch caught my eye. I slammed on the brakes, hoping I'd found my money that had slipped out of Ted's pocket, but no, it was a wad of trash, probably created by the dang raccoons. Next to it was a snakeskin.

Climbing back on Milly's bike, I thought of catching rattlesnakes for cash. Maybe sell them for meat and earn the rattler button bounty from The Oracle? But then I remembered a couple of weeks earlier when Mom found out we were going to do that for bait money. In what Preech later described as her "extreme negativity regarding the idea," she'd yelled so loud, it felt like my ears were still ringing.

I stood on the pedals, thinking how good it would feel to tell someone about Ted, to just get the words out of me. But I couldn't. Rudy would freak out, and Preech and The Oracle would probably tell me to call the police. Ted would tell them about the letter, and we'd all end up stuck in a cell somewhere. Plus, if Ted somehow found out and got away, my lucky rock would be gone forever. And no telling what the lunatic might do to Milly.

I got to The Oracle's. He and Rudy were tending a roaring fire at the brush pile. A mile-long plume of smoke slithered into the sky.

Preech had just finished feeding the chickens. He jogged to me, pulled off his work gloves, and smiled. "So, how'd everything go? Is it Smooch City at your place right now?"

I didn't have the heart to tell him what happened. "You wouldn't believe me if I told you."

Preech clapped. "Awesome."

"Do you still have any of your homemade itching powder?" I asked.

He held his thumb and finger a couple of inches apart. "About half a bottle. Need some?"

"Please." I was thinking of giving Ted a little bonus with his clothes once I found some.

He nodded. "Done."

"Thanks, man. Hey, remember when Kyle got his bell rung in football last year?"

"Do I?" Preech said. "That was bad. Doc called it the worst concussion he'd ever seen."

"Did he, like, see things that weren't there?"

"Dude, Kyle was all over the place. He's normally super nice, right? But when I stayed at his house to help look after him, he was all weird and mad, then happy, then super angry."

Wheels in my head started to click. "Interesting."

"Oh yeah, and he couldn't remember diddly what happened...like two whole days, totally gone."

"Ah-hah," I said. "So do you think—" Tires crunching on the crushed seashell driveway interrupted us.

Preech squinted at the car. "Whoa, who's that? She's smokin' hot!" He licked his palm and ran it over his hair.

"Dude, it's my mom."

"No, no, no—yuck—not your mom. Who's that with her?"

The glare on the windshield slid away. Behind it was someone who always made me happy, grinning and waving with both hands.

"Oh yeah, Tiff. My cousin Tiffany. Totally forgot she was coming. She's on spring break, too."

"Where's she from?"

"Montana."

"Big sky country, the land of shining mountains," he said. "And angels." Preech sprinted to Oliver's house. "Be right back. Make sure she doesn't go anywhere."

Walking to the car, I remembered what a good time it had been on our family camping trip to Colorado a couple of years earlier. I noticed the tan line on my mom's finger, where her wedding ring was supposed to be. Soul-crushing sadness sliced through me.

They'd barely stopped when the passenger door flew open and out bounced Tiff. Her Cracker-Jack-colored hair danced and flipped, and her cool green eyes shined brighter than the sun. She almost knocked me down with a full-on bear hug. "What up, cuz!"

"Hey, Tiff, how you been?"

"Excellent, thank you."

The back door opened, and a pile of stuffed animals and Milly spilled out. She leaned over, getting right in their faces. "What have I told you about staying in the car?" Milly picked them up, scolded each one for not minding her, and tossed them in the back seat.

Curi had come halfway from the brush pile, but stopped and stood with his head cocked, confused about the new arrival.

"What a good-looking girl!" Tiff dropped to her knees, making kissing sounds. "C'mon, come here, gorgeous."

Milly slammed the car door. "No, Tiff, Curi is a him. He's a him." She sat next to Tiff, mimicking her every move.

"Well then, come here, handsome boy!"

Milly tried to whistle. "C'mon over here, you pretty bag of fur."

Curi sped towards them, his tail wagging so hard I thought it was going to fly off.

Milly played and rolled with him. She left Curi with Tiff and skipped to me, and then latched onto my leg like a spider monkey. "What ya wanna do?"

I smiled. "Think we're gonna burn some stuff, go to the dump, and after that, clean some stuff up, go back to the dump, then eat caterpillars or something. Oh yeah, then we'll go to the dump."

She unlatched, stood, and pinched her nose shut. "The dump is no place for a lady."

"Works every time," I whispered.

Mom tapped the horn, pointed at Milly, then at the back seat, and nodded her head sideways for me to come talk to her.

Milly opened the door, and only one stuffed animal jumped out. She bent over, picked it up, and glared into the poor little giraffe's eyes. "Jeffery, how many times have I told you to not do that? You could break your head open." Exasperated, she stuck Jeffery in her armpit, climbed into the car, and mumbled, "What am I going to do with you?"

I walked to the driver's side. Boxes filled the back of the station wagon, crammed in so tight I doubted there was enough space to wiggle in a human hair.

Mom cranked the window down. "Hey hon, got some things I have to do. Can Tiff stay here for a bit?"

Unable to tear my eyes off of her naked finger, I nodded. "Umm, Mom?"

"Yes?"

Words tried to climb up my throat, but fear killed them before they got to my mouth.

The screen door slammed shut. Preech jumped down the stairs in one leap. He puffed out his chest and strutted towards us, his back as straight as a fishing pole.

"Nothing, never mind. See you later." I looked into Mom's wet eyes. A bolt of pain ripped through me.

"No matter what happens, remember I love you, buddy. We'll always have each other," she said, and the car flew backwards, turned around, and tore down the driveway.

I walked back to Tiff. She beamed. "Wow, what a spread."

Preech smiled and waved, and from four steps away, a cloud of Oliver's aftershave hit us. Had he used the whole bottle? Two, maybe?

"Why, hello." Preech shook her hand and bowed.

Tiff leaned back, scrunching up her nose. "Rudy?"

Preech coughed and sputtered. "Me? Heck no. Absolutely not. I'm amazed that dude makes it out of his house with his underwear on the right side of his pants."

She threw her head back and laughed.

He continued. "Rudy can eat ice cream as fast as he wants because he doesn't exactly have to worry about brain freeze, if you know what I mean."

"Oookaayy." Tiff grinned. "So that would make you Creech, correct?"

"Close. The name is Preech."

"Is that a family name?"

Frowning, he shook his head. "No, sadly that is not the case. It's a derivative of my real name, one that I will change the second I turn eighteen. I've checked the laws."

Tiff batted her eyelids. "Soo, what is your real name?"

"Ma'am, I can help you with just about anything, but not the answer to that question. My parents have a very twisted sense of humor."

"C'mon, can't be that bad," Tiff said.

"Only me, my family, and some governmental agencies know, and every year I have to bribe the teachers handsomely to not spill the beans."

She bumped me with her hip. "Have you told your friends?"

Preech shook his head.

"We're all best friends." I pointed at Preech, and then at Rudy down by the burn pile. He and The Oracle had their backs to us, watching the fire. "But those two have a—what someone might say—sort of interesting way of showing it," I said. "You'll see."

"Oh yeah." She smiled. "Aunt Connie told me all about the 'three amigos.' She said one's an athlete, one's a mathlete, and there's, well, there's you."

I let the words sink in, unsure if I should be offended or not. Gee whiz, my own mother.

"So, your mom is Kevin's mom's sister?" Preech asked.

Tiff nodded. "Yep, my mom, Kevin's mom, and Aunt Deedee are the three girls, and also their brother Darron. He's the coolest uncle ever."

"Well, that's just like, wow, umm, so, you know, swell."

I figured there were about three million words bouncing around Preech's brain, but I'd never seen a time when he couldn't find one.

There was a loud *whump!*

We looked towards the burn pile. A smoky fireball rose into the air. From half a football field away, I could almost feel the heat vibrating off of it.

Rudy held the long, forked push-stick over his head in triumph. The Oracle's deep belly laugh was so loud it was like he was standing next to us.

Preech clapped. "They must have hit the fire with one of my diesel depth charges to speed things up." He looked at Tiff. "You gotta meet my Uncle Oliver. He's the man, the myth, and the legend around here. Be right back." Preech did a half-bow to Tiff, excusing himself, ran a few steps, stopped to look back at her, and then sprinted to the burn pile.

Tiff grabbed my shoulders, pulled me close, and her eyes locked with mine. Her hair smelled like a catcher's mitt, and her breath like Fritos. I started to see why Preech was going all gaga over her.

"Kev, I talked to your mom about what's going on, and I want you to know—"

I raised my hand, cutting her off. Was it embarrassment? Shame, maybe? I wasn't sure, but all I knew was that I did *not* feel like jabbing a finger into that wound. "Thanks, but I don't want to, you know, think about that stuff."

"Gotcha." She hugged me. "I just want everything to be alright."

I nodded and watched the smoke pump out of the roaring fire. Preech was talking to Oliver, all excited, his hands flying everywhere. They turned and walked towards us.

The Oracle turned back around, pointed to the fire, and said something to Rudy. Rudy saluted him, waved at us, and turned to push brush into the blaze.

"Man, this place is great." Tiff leaned over to pet Curi, who kept so close it appeared his head was sewn into her jeans. Oliver and Preech got within a few steps. "An amazing place you have here, sir," Tiff said.

"Why, thank you, ma'am." He shook her hand and patted Preech on the back. "I've got the best posse in the county helping me keep things in order. Name's Oliver."

"Tiffany, Tiff is fine. I'm from Montana," she said, motioning towards the hog pen. "I don't think I've seen a bigger or happier pig."

Oliver grinned. "Yep, old Rosalynn gets a lot of beauty sleep and doesn't miss many meals. You can't fatten a hog on market day as they say."

Her eyes opened wide. "Exactly what my dad says!"

Oliver nodded his approval. "Sounds like a smart fellow."

"Oh yeah, he says kooky and clever stuff all the time. Calls himself Cornfucious. Says things like 'He who cuts his own firewood warms himself twice,' and 'There is no knowledge gained from the second time a mule kicks you.'"

Oliver laughed and lifted his cane towards the donkey. "Speakin' of that, the last place you want to find yourself is behind Pele there. First day I got him, I made the mistake of getting too close to his backside. He launched my peg leg about thirty yards into the pasture. Was a long hop getting it back, but you bet I learned quick he was born to kick."

I shuddered. The furry beast had terrified me from the second I'd met him.

"Uncle Oliver, show her the trick you taught him," Preech said.

The Oracle cupped his hands around his mouth and boomed, "Pele! Score!"

Pele swiveled his ears around, pulled up a leg, and whipped out a vicious kick, and then went back to chewing hay.

Tiff whistled. "Well, that's good to know, sir."

"Can we interest you in a nice cold drink, Tiff from Montana?"

"Yes, please."

"On it." Preech sprinted to the house.

Oliver pointed his cane towards the brush pile. "Think I'll relieve Private Rudy. Back in a bit."

Preech returned with five glasses of ice, ran back to the house, and emerged with five bottles of Dr Pepper.

"Ooh." Tiff licked her lips. "What's this? Is it spicy?"

"You never had a Dr Pepper?" Preech asked.

Tiff shook her head. "I'm from a pretty small town."

"Dr Pepper is a sugary, sweet nectar straight from heaven." He whipped out a bottle opener and peeled the cap off of Tiff's bottle.

She took a sip. "Yum!"

"Oh, wait." Preech ran around the barn and came back with two freshly picked flowers. He set them in front of Tiff and sat down.

She grinned. "Why, thank you."

The smell of smoke surrounded us as Rudy reached the picnic table, trying to nudge Preech down the bench.

Preech dug his fingernails into the wood, not about to give away the spot across from Tiff.

She waved. "Hi there, I'm Tiff."

"Howdy." Rudy stared at the table. "Glasses? With ice? What's up with that?"

"Well," Preech said, "those of us *not* raised by baboons enjoy a little couth now and then."

Rudy took the seat across from me. "Whatever."

Tiff poured all the Dr Pepper she could into her glass, drank the rest, and laid the bottle sideways on the table. Her eyebrows danced up and down. "I've got the best game for us to play. Here we go."

The bottle wobbled and bucked on the old wood. Preech lit up like a fireball when it stopped spinning, aiming at him.

Tiff leaned across the table, and Preech, with the dopiest yet happiest look I'd ever seen, eased out of his seat to meet her halfway.

"Okay, Preech, or whatever your name is, what scares you the most?"

After a few awkward seconds, Preech opened one eye, unpuckered his lips, and slumped back into his seat. "Clearly I've been misinformed about this game."

Rudy snickered.

"What?" Tiff asked. "You've never played Bottle of Truth before? We play it all the time."

"Nope," Preech said. "Nuh uh, never heard of it."

"The spinner gets to ask any question they want. Like what makes you happiest, who you'd most like to be stranded on an island with, what body part you'd hate to lose the most, all kinds of stuff."

Preech scratched his chin. "Well, okay then, the answer is blue ice."

"Aww, man, here we go again," Rudy hooked his thumb at Preech. "Every time a plane flies over, Egg Head runs for the trees. Totally lame."

"What would be worse than getting smeared by a half-ton of frozen—"

Preech looked at Tiff. "You know, umm, human waste. It'd be like the most horrible last second of your life to see that a foot above you, falling at terminal velocity like the silent assassin of nastiness."

"Whoa." Tiff spun the bottle again. "Scary and disturbing. Two bonus points to you. Here we go again."

As the bottle spun and skipped on the table, I wondered what my answer would be if it landed on me. There were two things in a dead tie for scaring me just about every second of my life, and there was no way I could talk about either one.

Thankfully, the bottle stopped on Rudy.

"Okay, superstar. Scariest thing," Tiff said.

"Old Man Perkins' place." Rudy's voice dropped to a whisper. "So we're all going there. Tonight."

CHAPTER 13

I tried to speak, but it felt like Pele had donkey-kicked every molecule of air out of me.

One of Preech's eyelids started to twitch, a sure sign he was about to freak out. If he knew Ted was there, I figured it'd start flapping so fast it might fly right off his face.

"You okay, Mathlete?" Tiff asked.

Preech covered his eye with one hand and pointed at Rudy with the other. "I'm fine, probably smoke coming off the Sasquatch or dust or something. Be right back." He pushed off the table and took off towards Oliver's house.

Tiff tapped Rudy's arm. "So, Kev tells me you three are best friends. What's Preech's story?"

Rudy shrugged. "Preech is a weirdo."

Tiff grinned. "How so?"

"Well, for starters, the dude reads dictionaries for fun, puts mustard on his pizza, and says messed up things like 'I wonder what they called electric eels before electricity was invented' and 'lightning comes from the ground up' and 'you think we'd mow grass if it screamed when we cut it' and 'you never step in the same river twice.'"

Tiff rubbed her chin. "Wow, that's deep."

Rudy frowned. "What, the river?"

She shook her head. "No, the meaning. We're always changing, and a river is always changing, so it's impossible to ever step in the exact same river more than once."

"Whatever," said Rudy.

Oliver whistled from the brush pile. Preech changed course and headed towards it. Oliver left Preech to tend the fire, walked up to the picnic table, and asked, "Y'all haven't seen a pocket watch around here, have you?"

We looked under the table and around it.

I shrugged. "No, sir."

"Would you mind fanning out and searching the yard? And could I get a hand looking inside?"

Tiff's arm shot up. "Will do, sir. You sure have the heat cranked up down here. I think the high in Montana today is only sixty."

"This is nothing." He chuckled. "Come back in August and you'll have to wear shoes with brick soles."

Oliver and Tiff headed to the house. He said something that made her laugh the whole way there.

Rudy and I walked next to each other, scanning the grass for the watch. "Hey, Big Cat, what you said about Old Man Perkins' place, do you think—"

He shook his head. "I was joking. Not that I'm chicken or anything, but from what I've heard, I wouldn't go out there without riding in a tank carrying a hundred gallons of holy water."

"Yeah, okay, great." My stomach twisted at the thought of having to go back by myself.

As we finished searching the yard, the screen door screeched open. Out walked Oliver, carrying a pair of overalls.

"I believe I've deduced what happened." He ran his hand up the leg, and his fingers appeared through the hole in his pocket. A wave of dread swept over me as he wiggled his fingers through the cloth, reminding me of Ted's from earlier.

"Last time I remember winding it was when Curi and I secured the perimeter before y'all got here this morning." Oliver walked to the water spigot sticking out of the side of the house, and whistled at Preech.

Preech cupped his hands behind his ears. Oliver pointed to the fire and hollered, "Let's put it out, private."

Preech saluted and grabbed a hose attached to five others stretching from the house to the burn pile. Oliver cranked the handle. After a bit, water poured out of it. Preech sprayed down the fire.

Rudy's eyes lit up. He walked to the spigot, turned the water off, and dove around the side of the house. The water stopped flowing. Preech whipped the hose, like he was working out a kink. Rudy laughed. "Let me know when he looks *inside* the hose."

Preech lifted and held the hose over his head, then shoved a stick into the end.

"Now," I said.

Rudy jumped up, ran around the house, and turned the spigot back on. Water spewed out, dousing Preech, who shook his fists, yelled at Rudy, and then turned the hose back on the fire.

Once it was out, Rudy cut the water off. Preech stomped the ashes to make sure.

"Private Rudy and Miss Montana, would you two be so kind to help me scare up the snake boots? We can stuff some socks in the toes of mine for you to wear." The Oracle gestured to Tiff.

They followed him to the house.

Preech jogged to me. The cloud of smoky aftershave surrounding him pushed me back a step. His mini-shower had done little to knock it out. "Where'd Tiff go? Did she ask about me?"

"Inside, getting snake boots. And no."

"Okay. Hey, I'm less than positive about going to Old Man Perkins'. The way I see things, if you have to stop and ask yourself if something is a bad idea, it is."

"No worries, bro." I patted his back. "Rudy was bluffing."

The screen door creaked open.

Preech hit the grass and started doing push-ups. As Oliver, Tiff, and Rudy approached, he counted out, "Ninety-nine, one hundred." He jumped to his feet and sniffed. "Yeah, I work out."

Tiff grinned, Rudy rolled his eyes, and we swapped our shoes for the boots.

She tapped the toe of hers before sliding it on. "I hear about a rattlesnake now and then in Montana; think they call them prairie rattlers. Do you have a lot of snakes here?"

"You bet," Oliver said. "We're covered up with diamondback rattlesnakes, cottonmouth water moccasins, coral snakes, and if you smell something like cucumber in the woods, you may have riled up a copperhead, so look out where you step."

"Wow, will do."

"We can double-time it by splitting up and starting at opposite ends of the trail. Should meet somewhere in the middle." Oliver yanked a stalk of Johnson grass about as thick as a pencil out of the pasture. He pulled out his pocketknife and pointed his chin at the house. "Private Rudy, why don't you go grab the walkie-talkies. We'll draw straws to see who goes with which unit."

Rudy saluted and took off.

Oliver cut the grass into five pieces, all the same size, and then cut two shorter. After mixing them up behind his back, he offered them to Tiff. "Ladies first." After she pulled one out, he said, "Private Preech, you're up."

Preech slid one out and compared his to Tiff's, both long. I heard him say a quiet "Yes!" as he walked away.

I eased one out. It matched Tiff's.

Rudy returned with the walkie-talkies and handed one to me.

"Let's move out, troops. Rudy, you're with me."

We got to the woods and separated into two groups. Curi danced and barked, running back and forth between us.

"Poor thing," Tiff said. "Looks like he's trying to split in two and go with both of us. What a great dog."

Curi chose Oliver and Rudy, clearly unhappy we hadn't all stayed together.

Just before disappearing into the trees, Oliver pointed to the walkie-talkie in Rudy's hand. "Testing," crackled Rudy's voice.

"Roger that, loud and clear," I said as I walked backward down the trail. "What's your handle? Over."

"Dark Eagle. What's y'all's gonna be? Over."

Preech grinned. "I'll take that, thank you."

I handed the walkie-talkie to him. He rubbed his chin and pushed the button. ""Ours will be Treasure Finders."

After a few steps, Rudy's voice shot out of the walkie-talkie. "Dark Eagle here. Find anything yet? Over."

"Nothing here yet, Dead Weasel, but I smell you loud and clear. Anything on your end? Over." We cracked up as he let go of the button.

"Listen, we're on a mission to help Oliver, so stop the monkey business, got it? I repeat, this is Dark Eagle, anything yet? Over."

Preech pushed the button. "Negative, Drunk Beagle, nothing here. Anything on your end? Under."

Tiff bumped me with her hip and whispered, "Is this how they act all the time?"

I nodded. "Oh yeah."

"Whose side are you on?"

I held up my hands. "Neither. No way. Besides, me and Oliver took a blood oath that we'd help them sometimes, but never pick a side. If they ever combined forces, it could be apocalyptic."

Preech was laughing so hard, his face had turned as red as a fishing bobber. "Dung Beetle, Treasure Finders here. Thought I found your brains, but it was a cow pie. Anything on your end? Over."

"Dark Eagle here. Next time I see you, I'm gonna pound you as flat as a cow pie. You already stink like one. Nothing here yet, over."

Tiff was a few steps ahead of us when Preech grabbed my arm, spun me around, and pointed just off the trail. Sunlight lit up a long gold chain.

CHAPTER 14

Preech bent over, gently pulled on the chain, and Oliver's pocket watch slid out from under a pile of leaves.

I sucked in a breath to call Tiff, but Preech put his finger to my lips and whispered, "I want *her* to find it." He set the watch a few feet in front of a small patch of bluebonnets, walked back to me, and cleared his throat. "Hey, Tiff, do y'all have these in Montana?"

She turned around and eased back towards us. "Any what?" Tiff stared in the direction he was pointing. Her eyes bugged out when she saw it.

Preech lunged like he was making a move for it. Rattlesnake quick, Tiff hooked his boot with hers. He landed with a thud, spreadeagled on the trail like a starfish.

Tiff put one boot on his back, one on his head, and with a loud "Ah ha!" jumped over him. She dove, hit the ground, rolled once, and came up with the watch in her hand. Holding it over her head, Tiff belted out a triumphant, "Woo-hoo!"

Preech's face was tattooed with dirt and pebbles. He scraped them off his tongue and whispered, "I'm in love. She's part Sacajawea, part Mother Theresa, and a dash of Bonnie, as in Bonnie and Clyde. The perfect woman."

The walkie-talkie screeched to life. "Dark Eagle here. Thought we heard something. Over."

Preech dusted off his hands and clicked the button. "Affirmative, Dork Weevil. The rock is in the sock. Mission accomplished." He winked at Tiff. "And the prettiest girl in Montana has eagle eyes. See you back at the nest. Over."

Rudy's voice screeched through the air. "You're gonna wish you were a dead weasel or whatever you've been calling me, because when I see you, I'm going to—"

Preech clicked off the power button and sighed. "Enough of his monosyllabic mumbo jumbo. *You* are an excellent treasure hunter."

"Thanks." She turned the watch over in her hand. "Magnificent. Where'd your uncle get this?"

"Dunno." Preech shrugged. "He's had it for as long as I can remember. Sure will be happy to have it back."

We emerged from the woods. Curi met us with two licks each, actually four for Tiff.

Meeting up again, she handed Oliver the watch. He pulled a five-dollar bill from his wallet. "Thank you very much, ma'am. I truly cherish this thing. Here's a little something for your search and recovery skills."

"Oh, no, sir, I can't take that. It was my pleasure to help."

The Oracle shook his head. "I insist. I just wasn't myself without it. Please take it as a thank-you."

"No problem at all. Very generous, sir. Thank you."

As we continued towards the house, Tiff and I fell behind a couple of steps. She grabbed the back of my shirt and pulled me to a stop. Pressing the money into my palm, she whispered, "Hey, keep this and give it back to Oliver when I leave, okay? Such a sweet guy, but I figure he won't take no for an answer."

I nodded and slipped the money into my pocket.

Back at the picnic table, Oliver sipped his Dr Pepper. "Why don't you troopers hop out of the snake boots? It's my treat at the Busy Spoon for chicken fried steak and pecan praline pie."

"Fantastic," Preech said. "Or, as they call chicken fried steak in Germany, wiener schnitzel."

Rudy scowled. "What snizzle? Made out of what? No thanks, I'll stick with the noodles they make over there."

"Good. More for us non-Neanderthals." Preech snapped his fingers. "Hey, Miss Montana, I've built an unsinkable raft and haven't christened it yet. 'SS Tiffany' has a nice ring, don't you think? Would love for you to join us on its maiden voyage today."

With a half grin, she said, "Sounds great, but I have to, umm, help Aunt Connie with some things." She looked at me, and then down at the table. Her grin disappeared. "Next time, though. Thanks."

We traded the snake boots for our shoes. Oliver wound his watch.

"That's a fantastic timepiece. Where'd it come from?" Tiff asked.

"A wedding gift...from my wife."

"Oohh," she said, looking around. "Where is she? I'd love to meet her."

Oliver chuckled. "That makes you and just about everyone else here. We got separated during the war, and I only recently discovered she's alive. I've got people trying to locate her, but no luck yet."

He pulled the picture out of his pocket, super careful, like an original copy of the Constitution, and laid it on the table. You could still see her face through the five layers of plastic he'd wrapped around it.

Tiff smiled. "She's beautiful. What gorgeous eyes."

Oliver nodded. "I was fishing in Key West once and the sea was so flat you could've rolled a marble to Cuba. The color of the water that day was a close second, but I've never seen anything that can match it."

Tiff pointed to his camo top. "So sweet. You keep her picture in that pocket so it'll be closest to your heart?"

For the first time ever, Oliver blushed. "Never thought about things that way, but I reckon I do. Been across the pond a few times already." He pointed at us. "Planning on taking my posse this summer to expand the effort. Calling it 'Mission Marlena.' Heck, with your eagle eyes, we should see if your folks will let you go as well. We're going to need all the help we can muster."

Tiff slammed her fists on the table. Bottles danced, and I almost jumped out of my skin. "Oh my gosh, that is the most romantic thing ever! What's the first thing you'll do when you find her?"

"Have to admit, I've got a bit of apprehension." Oliver patted his stomach. "I was a flat belly like these three the last time she saw me." He tapped his fake leg with his cane. "And I filled out a younger man's uniform better than I could today."

Tiff jumped off her seat and ran to him. "Are you serious? You are one of the coolest, most genuinely nice people I've ever met. She's probably still missing you like crazy right this second."

"Besides," Preech said, "if you rearrange the letters in your name, it spells 'I love r.' Who wouldn't take that as an awesome sign?" He nodded his chin at Rudy. "A lot better than having a name like 'Duyr.' Sounds like a drunk rooster."

"If you think about it," Tiff smiled, "*your* name rearranged spells 'Chreep.'"

Rudy's arms shot in the air, and he laughed. "Yes, it does. Yes, it does! That is epic!"

"No." Preech's eyes crossed for a split second, and then slid back to normal. "Hmm, you appear to be correct."

Tiff tapped his arm. "Well, tell us your *real* name, and we can see where that goes."

"Yeah, cough it up, Fishface," Rudy said.

Preech shook his head. "Nope, sorry, no can do."

A car horn blared.

"Whoops, Aunt Connie. Didn't hear her pull up." Tiff hugged Oliver. "Would it be okay to take a rain check on lunch but come back out here tomorrow morning if I can get away?"

He patted her shoulder. "Absolutely, young lady. See you then."

Preech grinned. "That would be magical."

Rudy looked at me, rolled his eyes, and mouthed the word, "Magical?"

I shrugged and walked with Tiff to the car. She whispered, "Do you want to talk about, umm, you know, everything?"

I felt as if all the air in me was escaping, like a pufferfish out of the water. "Nah, wish I could, but I can't. Just can't."

She slid her arm around my shoulders. "Cornfucious once said, 'If you say you can't do something, it's pretty near a fact you aren't going to do it.' Let me know when you want to, okay?"

"'Kay."

"I'm staying at Aunt Deedee's tonight. Do you want to meet at her place first thing in the morning?"

I nodded.

As we got to the car, I saw Milly's pinched lips and wide eyes, shooting daggers from the back seat. She pointed at her bike, and then at me. "Take it home. Now!"

Pretending I couldn't hear through the rolled-up window, I cupped my hands behind my ears. "What? Jake's a gnome cow?"

Her head shook furiously, and she jabbed her finger at it. "Bike. Back. Now!"

"Ohhh, Mike is a black cow. Very cool." I smiled and gave her two thumbs-up.

The car pulled away. Milly's arms and hands flew around the back seat, obviously trying to make Mom turn around. I felt kind of bad, but with everything else going on, her bike was about the only thing working for me. I figured a shoe-box full of taffy or a bunch of new dolls with hair should do the trick once I got everything straightened out.

Walking back to the picnic table, I noticed Preech had taken a picture with Oliver's Polaroid and was fanning the floppy piece of plastic back and forth.

"Check this out," he said.

It was a fuzzy image of the letters "YO" he'd scratched in the dirt with a stick.

"See? It has double meaning. Yo is another way to say hi, and I'm gonna write 'All that's missing is "U" so hurry back!' I'll mail this to Tiff so it'll surprise her when she gets home."

Rudy sucked down the rest of his Dr Pepper, cranked out a five-second burp, and thumped the picture. "Wow, I've never met a real-life stalker before."

"Not stalking, bonehead. It's the age-old pursuit of romance. One must have brains and common sense, two areas in which *you* are bankrupt." Preech tapped Rudy's bottle. "Ooh, but that gives me an idea. I'll mail the letter with a case of those too. She'll love it." He looked at me. "Hey, bud, since shipping ain't cheap, I'll need the cash back sooner than later, cool?"

I gulped and nodded.

He checked his watch. "Why don't you grab it when you pick up your fishing stuff? We gotta move to snag some quality time on the island. Oh, and another thing—bring your lucky rock. I got a metal piggy bank shaped like a safe." He twisted his fingers in the air like he was working a dial. "We can use it to bury all of them on the island for safe-keeping."

"For once, not a bad idea, Poindexter," said Rudy. "I left mine in my pocket the other day. Mom freaked because it almost trashed the washing machine."

All my spit had dried up, so I just nodded harder, but instantly loved the idea. No lucky rocks meant no reason for Ted to get close to any of them.

I rode Milly's bike home. Pulling into the driveway, I could almost taste the sadness hanging like a fog around our little house. I sprinted into the garage, grabbed my fishing stuff, and ran back out as quick as I could. My cast net and tackle box fit in the basket on the front, but there wasn't a cool tie-down hook on her bike like Preech had invented for ours. So I tucked my pole under my arm like a jousting rod and took off.

At the pond, Preech was unloading stuff from his bike and a wagon tied to it, setting everything on the raft. "Hola, amigo, check this out." He reached into his backpack and pulled out a pack of Juicy Fruit. "Methinks that rat Rudy has been sneaking gum out of my stash, so I got a little surprise for him."

I laughed. "What'd you do?"

"Got the sharpest knife known to man, split a piece in half, and melted the stick of gum back together after I filled the insides with a very potent hot pepper concoction I invented."

"Was it hard?"

"Oh yeah. Burned through about twenty packs before I finally figured out how to bring my plan together."

"Which one?"

He tapped the piece with the wrapper top sticking up. "I put it on the end. You can have all you want, but make sure not to take that one."

"How'd you melt it back together?"

Preech grinned. "Let's just say I have to buy my mom a new iron...but it'll be worth the effort when I even the score for the hole prank. He got me good with that one."

A couple of weeks earlier, Rudy had let Preech borrow his metal detector and a pair of boots. What Preech didn't know was that they were steel-toe boots, and the detector lit up like a slot machine every time it got close to them. He dug for most of the day, producing a respectful hole deep enough for the three of us to stand in before he figured everything out.

We heard Rudy before we saw him, a *squeak, squeak, squeak* that got louder as he crested the hill. His tires wobbled like pizzas, and when he hit the brakes, his bike slipped, skipped, and bucked to a stop. He glared at Preech. "You call this fixed? I got halfway here and my wheels whacked out like they were going to fly off."

"Whoops," Preech said. "Such a fine ride; I didn't want to go too hard on it. One more trip to my fix-it laboratory and everything will be good as new."

"Better be." Rudy pointed at the stuff on the raft. "Man, looks like we're going for a week. What're those, limes?"

Preech nodded. "Yep, to beat scurvy, a wicked-awful disease sailors get. I read that we'll be okay if we eat citrus-rich food types."

"Good thinking, man," Rudy said. "Oh, hey, I'll load your backpack for you."

Preech winked at me. "What a guy. Thanks." He handed it to Rudy, and then pulled out the mini-safe piggy bank from the wagon, dug out his lucky rock, and set it inside.

Rudy did the same.

"Do you have yours and Oliver's?"

"Yep," I said, taking the small box from Preech, praying the plan I'd thought about the whole way there would work.

I took Oliver's out of my pocket, dropped it in, and looked at the water. "Hey, my shoe!"

Their heads whipped towards the pond, and super quick, I grabbed one of the lucky rocks out and jammed it in my pocket.

"Oh, never mind. Must be seeing things," I said. When they looked back, I dug it out, plopped it in with the rest, closed the lid, and spun the dial.

Preech cut his eyes at me as he took it and weighed it in his hand. Terrified, I thought he was going to open it, but instead he shrugged and set it on top of the other stuff.

I handed Preech my tackle box. He stepped on the raft, and it tilted sideways. Limes rolled everywhere. "Oh, no you don't," he said, catching them and placing them on the pile. "Back where you belong, you little foodgitives. Hey, Kev, can I use your cast net to secure all this for the ride?"

"Sure." I tossed it to him.

He spread it over everything, and tucked the weights as far as he could underneath. "Ha, a cast net cocoon."

Rudy and I nodded.

Preech handed me a jar with holes poked in the top that was filled with grasshoppers and worms. "I want you to be the first one to cast to the island, amigo, so keep your pole out." Next, he handed me an old medicine bottle that had a skull and crossbones drawn on the label. "Don't mix those up." He grinned. "Said you needed some extremely potent homemade itching powder?"

Rudy scowled. "Wait a minute. I remember that stuff."

"Oh yeah." Preech beamed. "Works great in jock straps too."

I twisted the top as hard as I could to make sure it was closed and slid it into my pocket.

"I got here early and cut those." Preech nodded towards three pieces of bamboo, about as long as pole-vaulting poles.

Rudy picked them up and handed one to me and one to Preech. I couldn't remember being more excited as we stepped on the raft, pushed away from the bank, and poled towards the island. As we eased over the water, Preech mumbled the words to "Keep on Loving You" by REO Speedwagon.

Rudy shook his head and grinned. "Hey, Paul McDorkney, what'd you do with the money?"

"What money?"

"The money your mom gave you for singing lessons."

"For your information, Barnacle Brain, I am an excellent singer and will become an excellent dancer so I can marry Tiff someday. Even though she's probably betrothed to some land baron that owns half of Montana."

Rudy laughed. "What?"

Preech spit in the water. "I can see his smug face now, sitting in a solid gold truck, sucking on a foot-long cigar. But I have a secret weapon." He patted the piggy bank safe covered by the net. "What he doesn't know is that I have a diamond the size of a chicken gizzard for her hand. Let's see him try to match that."

We coasted within casting distance of the island. Preech set his bamboo pole on the raft, lightly touched his fingertips together, and bowed. "It is time."

I quadruple-baited with two worms and two grasshoppers, and then zinged it in the middle of a fresh fish swirl a few feet off the bank. Before it hit the bottom, my line zipped sideways, the drag screamed, and my fishing rod bent like a question mark.

Preech slid next to me. "Man, look at it go! Fight it, Kev. Man, fight that sucker. Wish I'd packed the harpoon!"

"Yow! What the—? Mouth's on fire!" Rudy hollered.

He was on the other side of the raft, pinwheeling his arms, inching dangerously close to the spear tips.

The gum shot from his mouth, landed with a splat on Preech's forehead, and the world tilted sideways. We were suspended in midair, our side of the raft lifted out of the water, and the pull of the monster fish was the only thing keeping us from flipping over.

Preech fell on the pile in the middle. There was a sickening click, the trap door flew open, and the coffee-colored pond swallowed all of our stuff.

CHAPTER 15

Rudy jumped away from the edge, and the raft smacked back onto the water. The trap door slammed shut, barely missing Preech's fingers.

"My cast net!" I yelled.

"Our lucky rocks!" Rudy moaned.

"My new solar-powered calculator!" Preech wailed. He grabbed hunks of his hair and stared at the door. "We never flipped it back over. I specifically designed it to open upwards. Water pressure must be pushing it shut."

"A door?" Rudy screamed. "A freaking door? On a boat?"

"Well, technically, it's a raft," said Preech.

"Well, *technically*, we lost all of our fishing stuff, food, and what may be four diamonds the size of golf balls. How you gonna get it back?"

My line went slack. I reeled as fast as I could to get tension back on the hook. "Umm, guys, he's coming right at us." The beast got almost directly underneath us before taking a hard right, dragging the line across the sharp spear tips, slicing through it.

"Whoa." Preech grabbed the line and examined it. "That cat knew exactly what to do. They are most worthy adversaries."

I stared into the water, trying to look through the sunlight shimmering off of it. "Maybe he saw our stuff and it spooked him. How are we going to know where to look for it?"

Preech clapped. "Oooh, I got it. Triangulation! Like in the Boy Scouts' handbook." He whipped a pencil and wadded piece of paper out of his pocket, smoothed out the wrinkles on his knee, and scribbled a map of the pond on it. "See that stump in the water there? That's one point." He turned to the left. "And that clump of cattails is another."

He turned to the left some more and pointed to the bank. "The tree over there is the third. When we're at this exact spot again, we'll know we're on top of it."

I slid the push pole down until it hit bottom. "How long did you cut these?"

"Thirteen feet. Exactly."

"So everything is about ten feet down. How do we get it?"

"Easy," Preech said. "The masks and hoses we used for our treasure hunt in Florida when we found our lucky rocks. I think The Oracle still has them. We just gotta figure a way to retrieve it without being attacked by piranhas or snapping turtles or anything else looking for a snack."

"Or," I said, welcoming a surprise visit from my old friend, luck, "we pull it out."

Floating right under the water was the land line attached to my cast net. I slid the tip of my fishing pole through the loop and eased it out, but it caught tight a couple of inches out of the water.

Preech laughed. "Outstanding."

"Cool." Rudy grinned. "Haul it up."

"We better not." Preech latched and unlatched his fingers to form a finger basket. "If it's not wrapped tight on the bottom, everything may dump and scatter. Makes an excellent marker, though."

Rudy leaned so close to Preech, their eyelashes almost butterfly kissed. "Heyyy, what's in the gum? Are those pepper flecks?"

Gooey strings dripped down Preech's nose and shirt as he peeled it off of his forehead. "No time now, but, umm, I'll take this to my lab and do a full investigation."

"Uh huh," Rudy said.

Preech snapped his fingers. "Oooh, we need rope. How about you swim to shore and bring it back from our stump safe?"

Rudy pointed to himself. "What? Why me?"

"Kev's got to keep the land line hooked on his pole, I've got to keep us on top of it, and you're like a greased barracuda in the water."

Rudy shuffled towards the edge. "I don't think so. There's no telling—"

Preech hip-checked Rudy and sent him sailing off the raft and into the murky depths. "Whoops."

Rudy's head popped out of the water. Spitting and coughing, he shook his fist at Preech. "You're so dead." He started towards the raft, and stopped a few inches from the spears. "Great, there's no way I can climb back on."

"Better head out then, Big Guy. Good news is there're no sharks." Preech turned to me and whispered, "They hug with their teeth, you know."

"Alright, alright." Rudy swam towards the bank.

We watched him cruise across the water, climb out, slide the rock away, and pull the rope out of the stump.

"Hey, Kev, maybe you'll make enough selling your lucky rock to retire, like my uncle Roland in Florida. He lives on a golf course, and when a ball lands in his yard, he runs out and lays next to it like he's dead. The golfers' reactions are hilarious."

"Oh yeah, that'd be great." I wondered, if we got our lucky rocks back, how I could convince them mine had somehow slid out of the piggy bank. But thinking that way felt weird...wrong in some way. Like there was a better answer, and I just couldn't see it.

Rudy swam back, the rope coiled around his head and shoulders like a skinny anaconda.

Preech burst out laughing.

Rudy scowled. "This isn't funny. Might be snakes or gators in here, weirdo." A fat string of pond scum had attached just above his lips, giving him a long wiggly snot-colored mustache.

"Okay," Preech said, "I'm going to push us away a bit, ha, from the tips, ha, ha, and you tie it off but don't pull too ha-ha-haard." He wheezed, hands on his knees, trying to catch his breath.

I offered the tip of my rod to him, unable to stop a smile. He attached the land line to the rope, threw the rest of it onto the raft, and swam towards the bank.

After poling back, Preech tied the rope to a rock, and then took extra and secured it to the raft so it wouldn't float away. I squinted at the sun, figuring I had barely enough time to grab clothes and food and drop them off to Ted. Thinking of being at Old Man Perkins' after dark sent back-to-back shivers down my spine.

"Hey, Preech, since everything's so funky, I don't wanna stay at home tonight. Can I crash at your place?"

He nodded. "Sure. Might need some help on the plans for the recovery mission."

"After fixing my bike? The right way?" Rudy asked.

Preech gave him two thumbs-up. "Oh yeah, sure, you betcha. I'm all over it, like stink on a monkey. Tomorrow morning we can pick up the diving stuff at The Oracle's."

We walked our bikes up the hill. I hopped on Milly's. "Gotta go get some things. Meet you at your place later?"

"If you could grab my cash, it'd be great," Preech said.

I nodded. Every nod put a new knot in my stomach.

At home, Dad's truck was backed into the driveway, the bed full of more of his tools. In the garage, I found the garbage bag with worn-out clothes my parents usually took to the homeless shelter, threw it next to Milly's bike, eased the door open, and tip-toed into the kitchen. I heard Dad scratching around in the attic. A pile of boxes squatted on the floor by the ladder.

I snagged the sack of canned food and aspirin from the night before. On my way back through the garage, I thought about leaving my favorite fishing rod, but got scared it'd disappear like everything else. So I kept it.

The pink tassels on Milly's bike whipped in the wind as I raced to beat the sun, watching it go down like a giant orange fishing bobber. I slid to a stop at the clump of trees by the road, opened the bag of clothes, and pulled the bottle of itching powder from my pocket.

I couldn't remember how much Preech said to use. A cupful?

So I poured it all in, tied the bag shut, and shook and spun it for maximum coverage.

I crammed it back in the basket, and a corner of the book Ted had thrown at me peeked out from under the towel.

"Maybe the psycho will be in a trading mood," I whispered. Training wheels squeaked as I eased down the weed-covered dirt driveway. The shadows falling on the house made it look like a gigantic moaning mummy's head rising out of the earth. Fresh bike tracks and footprints crisscrossed next to the front steps.

I heaved the bag of clothes and the sack of food through the hole where the door used to be, and then jumped back lest something popped up and dragged me to the center of the earth.

I walked to the window on the side of the house. The radio was on. Hank Williams Jr.'s song "Family Tradition" floated out of the hole in the glass. In the middle of the room sat Ted—humming along and cradling all four of our lucky rocks in his arms.

CHAPTER 16

Ted smiled. Nasty green flecks dotted his teeth. "Looky here. I struck it rich!"

"What? How?" I asked. Preech and Rudy's fishing poles and our tackle was flung around the room. Next to him sat the mangled piggy bank safe, Preech's favorite hatchet propped against it.

Ted nudged his chin towards the back of the house. "I heard y'all squealin' like stuck pigs, so I went to shut yer yaps and nobody was there, but I did find me a magic rope headin' into the water."

He tossed our lucky rocks back into the piggy bank, and then made a pulling motion with his arms. "I drug it out, and just like that, I'm on easy street."

I checked the map of the county in my head. Even though the pond and Old Man Perkins' seemed to be far apart, they actually backed up to each other. If it weren't for the stretch of trees that ran along the fence, I figured you could see the water from the back porch.

"Drug it?" I said. "Did it tear up my cast net?"

He shrugged. "Prob'ly. But if you done your job right and got me two shoes, I wouldn't have got all tore up on the way back." He lifted his foot. It oozed with scratches and scrapes.

I stared down at fresh tire prints in the dirt. "I brought you food and clothes. Any chance of, umm, trading, sir? My bike maybe?"

"My momma didn't raise no fool." He hooked a thumb over his shoulder. "You gotta ask whatshisname about your precious little bike, but it would take something awful huge for me to part with anything else."

I looked where he pointed, saw nothing, and made a mental note to ask Preech how long concussions lasted.

Ted snorted. "Well, since you brought me grub..." He grabbed something off the floor and eased his fist through the hole in the glass.

I opened my hand, and into it dropped a half-eaten lime.

"Trading shack is closed." Ted smirked. "Now fetch me some shoes, then we can talk about getting some of your fishing junk back."

I chunked the lime into the brush, wiped his slobber off on a tree, and climbed on Milly's bike. I was almost to the road when Ted's voice ripped down the driveway. "Runt, back here, now!" He stood in the doorway, waving frantically for me to come back. It looked like the mummy had eaten a hot pepper, and its tongue was going nuts.

I pedaled back, and through the skinny daylight I could see panic in his eyes from twenty steps away. The clicking noise from his handcuff filled the woods. He jabbed his finger towards the radio. "Just heard on the squawk box they're gonna restart the search. I gotta lay some miles between me and here."

"Oh?"

He pointed to his bleeding foot. "And thanks to you I can't hoof it so you owe me some wheels. Pronto."

"Like my bike?"

"You got spit for brains?"

"Umm."

"Need a car. Truck would be better. The pinhead cops showed their cards, but," he tapped his forehead, "once you got the facts, Jack, you're unstoppable." He staggered down the steps and stopped a few inches from me. His body odor, mixed with the rotten rat-gut breath, made a glob of vomit rocket up the back of my throat.

He plucked Tiff's five-dollar bill out of my pocket. "I'll take that."

I reached for it. He balled the money into a fist with one hand and grabbed my shirt collar with the other. "Only gonna say this once. If I hear the cops or anyone else, every last bit of that fancy fishing equipment gets smashed, your precious little net gets caught on fire, and I guarantee you'll never sniff those stones again. And I'll tell the world what that punk Rudy done to me. Betcha he's gonna get twenty years for that."

He yelled the word "guarantee." Chunks of lime pelted my face.

"Ted, sir, I'm not sure where to find a truck or—"

He turned and limped up the steps. "Not my problem. If I don't have some wheels here by tomorrow, I'll crawl to town if I have to and hunt you down. You reckon either one of us wants that?"

I gulped, shook my head, and then rode down the driveway and onto the road.

On the way to Preech's, I thought about wheels. I couldn't do that to Dad, and it seemed like Mom and her station wagon were pretty much gone so that was a no go. Besides, I'd never driven a car or a truck. Pretty sure I could start it, but then what?

Gotta tell Preech, I thought. Things had gone way off the rails, and he'd have an answer. The dude could build a truck overnight if we needed it bad enough.

Light poured from Preech's garage onto the driveway. He was in his lab coat, wrenches poking out the pockets, and his cool magnifying glasses sat perched on his nose: a genius mechanic doing his thing.

Rudy's bike was flipped over on the work bench, sprockets and bike guts scattered everywhere.

I parked Milly's bike and set my fishing pole against the basket.

Preech pointed his screwdriver at the door. "Evening, amigo. Would you snag us some Cokes?"

"You got it." I walked inside to the kitchen and grabbed two out of the fridge.

Back in the garage, Preech stood next to Milly's bike, holding the book that had almost scalped me; like moths to a flame, if there's a book in the room, it's gonna find Preech. I smiled and offered him one of the cold bottles.

He jumped back, staring at me with a look on his face I'd never seen before. Horror? Disgust? Disbelief? A mixture of all three? His finger ran down the signatures inside the front cover. "The governor, mayor, all the important city figures. They say what took forever was getting it signed by Tom Landry *and* Willy Nelson." He threw it back in the basket, like it had burned his hand. "Dude, that's stolen. Everybody's looking for it and the other stuff from the time capsule. I'm all about fun and games, but I can't get wrapped into something like that."

I tried to find words but couldn't. All I could do was blink.

"I didn't want to say anything in front of Rudy, but I saw what you did with the lucky rocks at the pond today. What's going on? It's like you've totally changed, man."

The sweat from the bottles ran off my hands and dripped onto the concrete floor.

"And I know you've been lying about your bike, Kev." His voice cracked. "Please, tell me what's going on. Please."

I stood there, unable to speak or move. It was unreal, like I'd left my body and was watching the horrible train wreck from above. Thoughts of Ted shot through my head: smashing all of our stuff, catching my cast net on fire, showing the police where we lived to come and take us away.

Preech's chin quivered. "Listen, might be best if you go home. Rudy and I will haul the stuff out tomorrow. He'll drop yours off."

I nodded, set the Cokes on the garage floor, put my fishing rod under my armpit, and turned the bike around. At the end of the driveway, I stopped to look back. A tear rolled down his cheek as the garage door slid shut, cutting us in half.

I walked alongside the tiny bike, replaying what happened, trying to figure out how everything got so bad so fast. A stone about the size of my lucky rock sat in the middle of the road. I gave it a kick and watched it skip down the street until it landed on something just out of the ring of light from a streetlamp. The stench of death was thick around a tire-flattened squirrel pelt, deader than my parents' marriage. Leaning over, I said, "Bummer. Which one of us has it worse you think—," Forgetting I was carrying my favorite fishing pole like a jousting rod, the nauseating sound of it snapping in half echoed up and down the empty street.

"Nooooo!" I howled to the moon and stars, and then jammed the shattered pieces into the basket and continued my walk of shame.

Nobody was home, so I pulled Milly's bike into our dark garage, locked the doors, and walked into an even darker house. Everything good or fun was gone…like a humongous empty piñata. I shoved the book into the back of my underwear drawer and fell into bed. My body hurt, my heart hurt, but sleep wouldn't come, so I stared into the inky black air until it hit me: the tree house.

I grabbed my pillow and blanket and headed to the back of the yard and the place where I'd never, ever, had a problem, like it had some cool force field, constantly pushing back any bad times that tried to penetrate it. I stretched out on my blanket and counted stars, then counted everything I'd lost.

Favorite fishing rod? Check. The new red Camaro I was going to buy Mom to replace her old dragon wagon with the diamond money? Poof. Astronaut pens and pencils for Dad, so he could draw his cool buildings and homes upside down if he wanted to? Gone. Every Barbie and Barbie doll accessory ever made for Milly? Disappeared into the biggest sinkhole in the history of the earth. The awesome floating cabin I was going to build on the pond, complete with a trap door (that opened upwards) in the floor, so I could fish day or night, rain or shine? That dream spit the hook and swam away forever.

But what hurt worse than anything was, no more Preech. It felt like losing an arm. I tried to block the thoughts of him, because every time one popped into my brain, I couldn't breathe. But like ferocious punches, they kept coming.

I could still smell his singed hair from the time he amped up the booster propellant in his Estes model rocket. Immediately after takeoff, it did a loop-de-loop, barely missed his head, and left a reverse Mohawk burned onto his scalp.

And the day he laughed so hard milk shot out of his nose when he convinced Rudy to put a sheet on his bike like a sail during a windstorm. We figured he set some kind of land speed record before his wheel flew off. Would I have to start reading a dictionary to get a "word for the day"? How weird.

Rudy was great, but it'd never be the same. Everything was better in threes: three musketeers, three amigos, three stooges, three-bean soup my mom made (or used to make). Everything.

CHAPTER 17

A loud, creepy, scratching noise floated out of the alley, snapping me out of my thoughts. Like a ninja warrior, I flipped over, eased up to a crouch, and peeked over the tree house railing.

The raccoons were back.

The whole family rolled and frolicked, giddy about creating the world's longest trash heap. Out of the corner of my eye, I spied another one, appearing and disappearing in the pools of lamp light that dotted the alley. He was different somehow—bigger, uglier, missing an ear, and did an off-balance wobbly sideways walk towards the others. One of the little ones noticed him first, stopped what he was doing, and squealed and chatted at the rest. They all stopped, too, tightened into a pack, and then screeched and waved their greasy paws at the newcomer. The conversation went back and forth for a bit, and then he turned around, hung his head, and shuffled away.

I lay back on my blanket and replayed the event: a young filthy-dirty little bandit told the older gutter gangsters about a potential problem, they banded together, and solved it.

Interesting.

Gray brush strokes slid across the sky, so I climbed out of the tree house, threw the pillow and blanket back in my room, and took off for Aunt Deedee's.

All of her house lights were on, and through the thin curtains I saw Mom, Dad, and Deedee sitting at the kitchen table, which made sense because both Mom's car and Dad's truck were there.

I took a step towards the house, and then froze, like my feet were suddenly welded to the damp grass. Part of me wanted to burst in there and scream—scream and yell and make them tell me what I'd done that made everything so bad, what I could do to fix it. It *needed* to be fixed.

But most of me said no. It was good to see Mom and Dad sitting together and not ripping each other's heads off, but the look of concern on their faces worried me. I wondered what they were doing. Were they in there, like playing a game of Risk, deciding who would have Milly or me on what weekend or holiday? Or figuring out who'd have to eat Dad's cooking, and if we'd have to start making our own clothes since me and him would never figure out the washing machine?

The thought of it made me sick.

The front door opened, and out slid Tiff. I got back on Milly's bike as she climbed onto Deedee's. "We tried to call you last night but no one answered. Aunt Connie said you could sleep through a tornado."

"You know it, yep, that's me," I said, and wondered if I'd slept at all the last couple of nights.

"Your mom and dad are both wanting everything—"

I raised my hand, interrupting her. "You know what I want Tiff? I want everything to go back to normal, how it used to be. Is that too much to ask?"

The first hints of sunlight wiggled through her hair. "Gee, I don't know, Kev. I don't know if it will ever go back to how it used to be."

"I know, I know. You're right," I said, and wondered if things would ever work out with Preech. "Sorry if I'm kind of snappy. Got a lot going on."

Her teeth gleamed in the fuzzy gray light. "Cornfucious says you get one-hundred percent of what you don't ask for, so what could it hurt, right?"

Suddenly, I felt a twinge of hope. Tadpole small, but I welcomed the nice, warm little buzz deep in my stomach.

We got to Oliver's, parked our bikes next to Preech and Rudy's, climbed the porch steps, and sat in chairs next to each other.

"You know," I said, "I've really been needing to tell–"

Tiff reached over and put her finger on my lips. "Shhh, I think I hear them coming."

Rudy's words drifted around the side of the house. "Thanks for bringing the pink medicine last night. Swelling's going away, but it still itches like crazy."

"Me, too," answered Preech.

The sound of his voice made my heart beat fast.

"Maybe next time we clean up poison ivy, we take off our gloves *before* we go to the bathroom."

"You think?" Preech said.

They rounded the corner carrying the water hoses and diving masks we'd used on our treasure hunt in Florida. When Preech saw Tiff, he skidded to a stop, dropped everything, and his whole head turned as red as a rash. "Oh my gosh, you didn't hear any of that, did you?"

Tiff's eyes opened wide. She bit back a grin. "Who me? Nope, nothing."

"Mortifying." Preech put his face in his hands.

Rudy shrugged. "Speakin' of pink, Coach Stark said they bought new football pants." He gave me a light punch on the arm. "Maybe this year yours will be the same color as ours, Kev Man. You know, instead of kinda pink like last year."

"If I even make the team," I said.

Tiff smiled. "It'd be cool if an NFL team made pink their official color."

Rudy shook his head. "Nope, no way, never gonna happen. No NFL player will *ever* wear anything pink."

Preech puffed out his chest. "I'll take that bet. What's the wager?"

Rudy rubbed his chin. "I'd eat a pair of my underwear."

"Clean or dirty?" Preech asked.

"One of each. Who cares? It will never ever happen."

"Deal." Preech extended his hand.

Rudy reached for Preech's, and then pulled back. "Wait a minute. What's in it for me?"

"Let's see." Preech tapped his lips. "How about on my deathbed, I will say you are more of a man than I could have ever hoped to be."

Rudy grabbed his hand, and they shook. "Deal. Safest bet I ever made."

They looked at me. I raised my hand. "Witness."

Tiff laughed and did the same.

Preech nodded his head sideways towards our bikes and mouthed, "We need to talk."

Butterflies exploded in my stomach. I gave him a thumbs-up, and we walked down the porch steps. Once we were out of earshot, he said, "Listen, I owe you a King-Kong-sized apology for what happened in the garage last night. I went by your place to tell you how bad I felt, but nobody was home." His eyebrows danced up and down. "Your folks on a second honeymoon after the flower magic?"

"I wish."

"Well, I should have heard you out. I'm sure you have a perfectly reasonable explanation for a highly illegal—"

"Ted gave me the book." The words poured out of my mouth. "Threw it so hard it almost stuck in my forehead."

"Ted? The janitor at school?"

"No, *the* Ted."

"Impossible. Ted's dead."

Telling someone felt good...I could almost taste the relief. But I was suddenly scared for Preech. Like knowing about it somehow put him in Ted's crosshairs. I shook my head. His eyelid shifted into twitch mode. "Is he in the river? All busted up, missing arms and legs and stuff?"

"Banged up for sure, but still in one piece. He's messed up in the head, though, staying at Old Man Perkins' place."

"What? You went out there? *Alone?*" Preech said, his voice going from a whisper to a half yell, and then back to a whisper. "Just you and him?"

"Yep, twice. Well, technically three times. Ted called me back to tell me—"

Tiff's head appeared between ours. "Who's Ted?"

I almost jumped out of my skin.

Preech's head whipped around. "Where's Rudy?"

"Helping Oliver with something in the house. What's up?"

"Okay," Preech whispered. "Ted is Rudy's dad, umm, stepdad, or ex-stepdad, and just about the most horrible person you could ever meet."

"Wow," Tiff said. "What does he do? Forget birthdays?"

I pulled her away from the house, so we could talk normally. "No, much worse. He's an escaped convict holed up in the scariest place on the planet, very stinky and demanding. And mean."

Preech wrapped his arm around my shoulders, which was so awesome it gave me goosebumps. "My main man here dealt with the psycho and battled ghosts and ghouls not once, not twice, but thrice. What a stallion!"

Tiff glanced back at the house. "What makes him so bad?"

Preech frowned. "Outside of the despicable things he did to Rudy and his mom, the maniac couldn't go a day without causing chaos. He'd do things like honk and wave at little kids on bikes hoping they'd wave back and wipe out."

"Rudy said he actually laughed at the end of *Old Yeller*," I said.

Preech pointed to the sky. "One time, when we were little, it was raining really hard and Ted told Rudy it was God crying, probably because of something he did."

Tiff shook her head. "Whoa, sounds like one dirty dog."

Preech nodded. "Indeed. As a human being, I give him two vigorous thumbs down."

I circled a finger around my ear. "And on top of that he's loco in the cabeza, has a huge nasty lump. He gets all mean, then kinda nice, then crazy mean again, sees things that aren't there. Weird."

Preech turned towards the house. "Let's call the police. Hopefully we can get there in time to watch them chunk him in the cruiser again!"

I grabbed the back of his shirt. "No way, no can do. He drug all of our stuff out of the pond, and if I don't get him some wheels today, he's going to smash it all. And he said he might hurt Milly."

Tiff dug her fingernails into my arm. "Oh, no."

"And what's even worse, Ted knows what Rudy—well, we—did with the letter. Said he was going to tell the cops, and that Rudy, and maybe me and you, will go to jail for it."

Preech's mouth hung open. "Whaaat?"

CHAPTER 18

The screen door screeched. Oliver walked out with his coffee thermos, and held the door open for Rudy, who was carrying a huge white cake on top of a stack of plates.

Oliver saluted us. "Morning, troopers."

We saluted back. "Good morning, sir."

He pointed his cane at the cake. "One of the nice town ladies brought me this yesterday, and I figure it has eggs, milk, and everything else a good breakfast should, so dig in."

I wasn't hungry but didn't want to let him down, so I sat at the picnic table. He slid toaster-sized slices to each of us.

Rudy tapped Preech's plate with his fork. "Hey, you figure out how we're gonna get our stuff out of the pond without turning into fish food?"

Cake crumbs spewed from Preech's mouth. His eyes shot back and forth between me and Tiff. "Whoops, sorry, umm, yeah, almost got it figured out."

The phone rang. Oliver climbed the steps and disappeared inside.

Thunder rolled, and the clouds bulged. I thought of what it would be like for Ted to have to dodge the hundreds of waterfalls that would pour in at Old Man Perkins' when it rained. My stomach curdled when I realized a decent chunk of the day had disappeared, and I was no closer to finding him wheels. Would he actually crawl into town to find me?

Oliver stepped out onto the porch. "Well, as you troopers say, I've got some bummer news."

Rudy raised his hand. "The alien mothership has decided it isn't coming back to take Preech home?"

Oliver stared out at the pond. It was weird seeing his face without a smile. "Negative. Just got word that an old friend of mine in Cleveland passed away. You can miss a wedding, but you never miss a funeral. Say they mailed a letter a while ago, but I never received it."

Everything went quiet. We looked at each other, and then back down at our plates.

I leaned over to Preech, and out of the side of my mouth whispered, "Think the funeral invitation was with Mr. Bernard? You know, during the raft and tire mishap?"

Preech rubbed his temples. "Oh, no. Man, I hope not."

"The challenge," Oliver said, "is that it's tomorrow, and the only way I can figure to get there is grab a red-eye flight out of Houston. Tonight."

"So sorry to hear that, sir, but Cleveland?" Preech asked. "That's *way* north."

Rudy nodded. "I hear people up there put beans in their chili."

That brought a weak grin out of The Oracle. He slumped into a chair. "Yep, I've spent a bit of time there. And trust me, never ask if their football team, The Browns, is named after the river that runs through the city. They become very angry if you do."

Rudy eased up from the picnic table. "Hey, my mom's been dying to go to Houston to pick up stuff to start a pottery hobby or something. Want me to see if she can go with you?"

"Thank you for the offer, private, but I couldn't impose like that. Wish Old Betsy had that kind of trip left in her, but I don't think she does."

I glanced at the tired, old ranch truck. It looked like Oliver had driven it through a meteor shower, and then Pele had kicked any square inch that wasn't scratched or dented.

"Where's your other truck?" Rudy asked.

"At the shop. Wheels off and a lot of work getting done on her."

Rudy headed inside. "I'll give her a quick call to see if you can borrow the car or something. Maybe you can pick the stuff up when you're there."

Tiff patted my arm. "Yes, sir, Oliver, I totally agree that you never miss a funeral. If it's only a couple of days, I bet these guys can handle things around here. I'll help, too."

Oliver scratched his chin and watched Curi nuzzle Tiff's palm. "I reckon my boy wouldn't miss any pats on the head, would he?"

Then—*boom!*—it hit me. I looked at Preech, nodded towards the truck, shrugged, and mouthed the words, "Ted's wheels?"

His eyes lit up. "We can handle everything around here, Uncle Oliver. I'll grab my notebook so we can write down everything we need to do." He ran to his bike.

I immediately felt guilty. What was I thinking? There was no way we could do that to Oliver. What kind of monster had Ted turned me into?

Rudy pushed the screen door open and put his palm over the bottom of the handset, its long, loopy green cord disappearing back in the house. "She's in, sir, and said if there's time, she'll take me down to Galveston for some salt-water fishing before you get back. She's got the rest of today and tomorrow off work and is heading home now to grab our stuff." He put his ear back on the handset, listened for a few seconds, and nodded. "She told me to tell you she won't take no for an answer."

The Oracle sighed and pushed himself out of his chair. "Well, can't thank y'all enough, but only if Daisy agrees I pay for gas and a nice hotel and dinner for you two tonight. I'll catch the first possible flight back to Houston after it's over tomorrow. Private Kevin, I'll call your folks, so they're aware of the developments, make sure they're okay with y'all looking after things for a bit."

It bummed me out to see him so sad, like the bad news had somehow made him smaller.

Rudy held the door open for The Oracle. "Hold on, Kev Man, what about the diving mission? You want me to stay and help instead?"

Something told me I needed to get Daisy and Rudy as far from Ted as possible. "Naw, it's cool. With the rain and all, we may delay it anyway. Besides, you already did most of the work by swimming the rope out there. We should be able to handle it."

Rudy pointed at Preech. "I guess we'll find out if there are any zombie fish in there. I hear they love weasel blood." The screen door slammed shut behind him.

Preech whistled and waved me and Tiff over. He was drawing furiously in his notebook.

"On second thought," I said, "I don't feel right about this. It's stealing, isn't it? From The Oracle of all people."

He shook his head and kept drawing. "You remember when he told us sometimes it's easier to get forgiveness than permission? Well, this is one of those times. Your idea was brilliant, but I took it up a notch...to help mitigate damage to Old Betsy." He showed us the paper. "Voila."

Written across the top of a map he'd drawn was "Old Man Perkins' and Vicinity." I was impressed at the detail that showed the house in the middle of the page and the area around it, complete with surrounding roads.

Preech grinned. "I can rig the gasometer to read full." He held his fingers an inch apart. "But it'll only have a little bit of gas in it. Once he takes off, we hightail it to the police and tell them which direction he went. If we help them nab an escaped convict, a stolen truck, and our stuff that's officially stolen too, maybe they'll go easy on us for the letter. Heck, there might even be a reward!"

"Letter? What letter?" Tiff asked.

Preech shrugged. "Well, we sort of helped Rudy get a letter that implicated Ted in some highly illegal yet untrue activities." He hooked a thumb at me. "Rudy planted it on Ted after this stud helped take him down with his lucky rock. It was a total David and Goliath scene."

"I don't know, Preech, man, it doesn't feel right."

Tiff stroked her chin. "Looks like our options are pretty skinny, cuz."

The clouds unloaded. The wind howled and a hard sideways rain peppered us.

Preech grabbed his notebook. "Whoa, it's a squall, people. Take cover!"

We ran onto the porch and shook along with Curi to try to dry off.

The screen door opened, and Oliver stepped out, in a suit.

"Wow," Tiff said. "Wherever you are Burt Reynolds, you've got some major competition."

For the second time ever, Oliver blushed. "Normally, I wear my Army dress greens for such an occasion, but it's getting a bit threadbare. Really want to keep it protected until I order a new one."

He tapped Preech's notebook with his cane. "What are you working on?"

Preech flipped through the pages. "Ummm, oh, uhh, let's see here. Oh yeah, our packing list for Germany. So far I've got you, me, Kevin, and Tiff. Not sure if there'll be enough room for Rudy the Sasquatch. May have to leave him behind, as to not freak out the villagers over there."

Oliver grinned. "I'm sure we can figure something out."

Tiff pointed at Old Betsy. "Oliver, sir, looks like your work truck sure has some character."

He nodded. "Affirmative. She's been very good to me. Don't know what I'd do around here without her." He tapped my knee with his cane. "Private Kevin, I called Connie to brief her on the situation. Said she's fine with it but didn't quite sound like herself. Everything alright at your place?"

Tiff and I looked at each other. Her eyes dropped to the porch.

"Family stuff, sir. Really hope they work things out somehow."

He leaned over. His face stopped a few inches from mine. "I'm not one to poke my nose where it doesn't belong, but I need you to know I'm all ears if I can help you or your family. Roger that?"

I nodded. "10-4. Roger that, sir." I didn't know if he'd said those exact words before, but for the first time, I'd *heard* them.

Daisy pulled up in her car. She jumped out, used a newspaper as an umbrella, ran through the rain onto the porch, and wrapped me in a hug. For the hundredth time, I wondered what kind of bamboozling trickery Ted had used to weasel his way into the world of someone so awesome.

Rudy appeared, carrying Oliver's suitcase. "Hey, Ma."

"Hey, buddy." She gave him a hug, and then gave Oliver one, too.

"Can't thank you enough for this, Daisy," The Oracle said. "I owe you one."

"Nonsense," she said. "I should be paying something for getting so much quality time with two of my favorite men on the planet." She smiled at Tiff. "Well, well, Kevin, do you have a new sweetheart you'd like to introduce me to?"

Preech coughed and sputtered, "Umm nope. They're cousins. Definitely no love interest between them. This is Tiff."

Daisy laughed and shook Tiff's hand. "Very pleased to meet you."

"Likewise." Tiff beamed.

"Speaking of sweethearts," Daisy touched the picture peeking out of Oliver's suit pocket, "the trip to Germany will be quite an adventure. Thank you again for including Rudy."

Oliver gave it a pat. "My greatest hope is that we achieve our objective."

The whisper of drizzle replaced the roar of the rain. Oliver nodded towards the car. "Looks like our chance." They ran and climbed in, and as they backed out, Rudy and Daisy waved goodbye. Oliver saluted us, and we stood at attention and saluted back. The second the taillights disappeared, Preech bolted off the porch, ran to the barn, and hurried back to Old Betsy, carrying a siphon, tube, funnel, and gas can.

CHAPTER 19

"It's go time, people," Preech said. "I think there's some gas in the lines and fuel system, so I'll drain the tank, then put in a half gallon or so. Should be plenty to get us there, but according to my calculations, Ted can only go a few miles once he takes off."

He pointed at the house. "Hey, will you grab me the super glue? In the drawer next to the kitchen sink?"

Preech put the tube into Old Betsy's gas tank and pumped the siphon bulb until fuel poured into the gas can. "Hey, did y'all know super glue was accidentally invented by a guy trying to make clear gun sights for the military?"

"You are just overflowing with useful information, aren't you, Mathlete?" Tiff said.

Preech beamed.

I found the glue and took a quick look around The Oracle's house. Even though it was constantly surrounded by dirt and pollen and stuff, it amazed me that I'd never seen a speck of dust inside.

I met Preech beside Old Betsy. He measured gas in a coffee can, poured it back into the tank through the funnel, and nodded. "That should do it."

Preech twisted on the cap, climbed into the truck, and took the tube of glue from my palm. Pulling a screwdriver out of the glove box, he said, "It's a good thing the glass from the instrument control panel is long gone. Would've made it trickier if it was still around." He used the screwdriver to push the fuel gauge to read full, squirted it with glue, counted to twenty, and slowly eased the metal tip away. "Perfect, but we gotta remember to fix this later. I'll go detach everything from my bike. I say we load them up to stash somewhere close to Old Man Perkins' so we can get back to town quicker."

I picked up his pencil and stabbed it in the spot where the driveway met the road. "There's a clump of trees and brush right here. That should work."

He smiled. "And they call *me* the genius."

Tiff and I helped each other get Milly and Deedee's bikes in the truck bed. Preech left an impressive pile of stuff in the garage and rode his bike to Old Betsy. He loaded it up with ours, ran to the passenger side of Oliver's truck, opened the door, and bowed to Tiff. "Your chariot awaits, mi'lady."

She rolled her eyes, grinned, climbed in, and slid to the middle of the seat. "How cute, like tiny bunny heads." She touched the white puffs of cotton that poked out of the cracked, sun-bleached fabric.

"While I'd love to have you riding shotgun next to me, it may be better to have Kev in the middle."

"How come?"

Preech ran around to the driver's side, grabbed the seat belt, and fingered the metal clasp. "The Oracle uses these for bottle openers and wore this one and the middle one out. The seat over there should be safest; that one still works."

Tiff nodded. "Okay, thanks."

I took the middle of the seat. Preech climbed in and turned the key. The engine roared to life, Old Betsy crept forward, and the tires crunched on the driveway as we eased from the crushed seashells to the asphalt.

Preech motioned ahead of us. "We better go back road, Joe, instead of through town. Might take a bit longer, but I'd like to protect the innocent bystanders."

We pulled up to a blinking red light. The shriek of squealing tires filled the air. I flew off the seat; my head ricocheted off the dashboard. The engine revved, and I flew back into the seat. A string of multi-colored bursts exploded in front of my eyes, like a roman candle had gone off in my head. A split second later, Preech stood on the brakes again. I shot off the seat, barely able to put my hands up before slamming into the hard metal a second time.

Tiff's words worked their way through the ringing roar in my ears. "Umm, Preech?"

"Yeah?"

"I'm pretty sure you only have to stop once at blinking red lights. At least that's how it works in Montana."

He chewed on his bottom lip and stared out the windshield. "Oh, okay, good to know. I didn't want to draw any extra attention to us."

"So, have you driven a lot?" Tiff asked.

Preech's hands made a weird squeaking noise as he gripped the steering wheel. I wondered if his were sweating as bad as mine. "The words 'a lot' are quite subjective. I've driven stuff around the farm for Uncle Oliver, but never on a real road...until now."

"Um, hmm." Tiff nodded and shoved the seat belt buckle in harder.

Trying to blink away my double vision, I said, "So the pedal on the right is gas, and the sideways one is the brakes?"

"Correct," answered Preech. "I use word association. The one on the right stands for really fast, and on the left stands for lethargy, or let's slow things down a bit."

Just before we got to Old Man Perkins', Preech parked off the road next to the clump of trees. We jumped out, yanked the bikes from the back, and I climbed behind the steering wheel.

Preech leaned into the cab and whispered, "Watch the brakes; they're very touchy for such a vintage ride."

I rubbed the knot growing on my forehead. "You don't say."

Tiff, Preech, and the bikes disappeared into the brush.

When I pushed on the pedal, the engine revved, but Old Betsy didn't move an inch. I pushed harder. Nothing.

Noticing the long shiny metal thing sticking out next to the steering wheel, I pulled it down and Old Betsy shot backwards. I took my foot off the gas and jammed both feet down hard on the brake pedal. Skidding to a sideways stop in the middle of the road, the stink of burned rubber and motor oil filled the truck.

"Hmmm," I said, looking at the "R" that the needle was stuck on. "Must stand for really fast backwards."

I pulled it down one more click, took my foot off the brake, and lightly pushed on the gas. So "N" stood for nothing? Not going anywhere? I pulled it one more click down, and the truck crept forward. To be safe, I stepped on the brakes, tied the seat belt into a knot around my stomach, and then eased my foot down on the gas.

I turned onto Old Man Perkins' place and stepped harder on the pedal. Brown and green blurs flew by the windows. My stomach told me we did two, possibly three, loop-de-loops before coming to a sideways stop a few feet from the porch steps.

Proud I hadn't killed myself, I pushed the metal stick all the way up, turned the keys backwards, and listened to the engine go from rumbling to quiet. I untied the seat belt, climbed out of the truck, and spied the curve of something familiar peeking around the side of the house.

My heart beat faster with every step as I turned the corner.

There it was: my bike! I hugged it and walked it back towards Old Betsy.

Ted stood on the porch, chunking our fishing gear, the bag of clothes, and cans of food into the truck.

He stopped every few seconds for a furious bout of scratching, reminding me of a gorilla I saw at the San Antonio zoo. I shivered when I remembered there was five-inch-thick glass that protected me from it, but only a few footsteps separated me from Ted.

"Good thing you finally did something right, maggot. Dang chiggers have gone nuts out here." His voice was mumbly, like his mouth was full of marbles. Ted shook his head at Old Betsy. "If I had more time, I'd take you to the woodshed for bringin' me such a hunk of junk. Consider yourself lucky, punk."

I nodded.

Peeking inside Old Man Perkins', I saw my cast net, the empty time capsule lying on its side, and a mostly empty bottle of human anti-freeze.

Ted grabbed the net and carelessly dragged it across the floor, snagging on every splinter and nail possible before he threw it in the back of the truck. He blinked at my bike, surprised to see it. "Where'd *that* come from? Load it up; should be good for a few bucks at a pawn shop."

I thought about grabbing my cast net, hopping on my bike, and tearing off into the woods. Then I remembered he wasn't going to get far on a few drops of gas, and very soon we'd be getting it all back. He limped out of the house with the mangled piggy bank. I cringed at the tinkly cry of our lucky rocks inside when it hit the passenger side floorboard.

Ted turned towards the house, cupped his hands around his mouth, and yelled, "Hey, dude, buggin' out in one minute. With or without you."

I walked to the side window and looked through the holes in the walls. Nothing but dirt, trash, weeds, and the time capsule.

On the way back to Old Betsy, an odd feeling about Ted came over me. Was it pity? Had I started to feel sorry about his mental situation? Either way, the sensation immediately disappeared when he said, "Yer too ugly to pass as my boy, so let's call you my neighbor's kid."

"Umm, what was that, sir?"

"Since that other feller done took off, you might come in handy if we meet up with the cops. We'll say we're on a fishin' trip."

"Well, uhh..."

He stroked his chin and looked me up and down. "May need a shield if they start shootin'."

I thought fast. "Okay, sir, sounds like an option, but wouldn't you need me to stay and figure out the letter situation?"

His hands balled into fists. "You *still* ain't taken care of that?"

I gulped. "I'm close, sir. Just been a bit hectic getting everything for you."

He opened the truck door. "You got one week. Let things simmer down around here and I'll be back."

"I'm on it, sir. Where might you be heading?"

"None of your business. Next time I see you, you better have good news for once." He climbed behind the wheel. "Outta here." Ted cranked up Old Betsy, stomped on the gas, and her engine screamed. Mud spewed out from behind the back wheels like rooster tails, coating me and the front porch.

I raked the mucky gunk out of my eyes. When they blinked clear, I saw the truck slip and slide down the muddy driveway. It gained speed and raced directly for the trees hiding Preech and Tiff.

CHAPTER 20

I took off running towards them. "Look out; he's coming right at you!" A second before impact, two blurs darted out of the brush and across the road.

The truck smashed into the trees. Leaves scattered as a loud, metallic crunch filled the woods. The driver door eased open, and Ted poured out of the truck into the weeds.

I ran as fast as I could and got there just as Preech and Tiff appeared.

Wide-eyed, Preech opened the passenger door, reached over, and turned off Old Betsy.

Tiff walked next to me and looked at Ted. "Call an ambulance—his brains are coming out of his head!"

"Oh, that. He's had that for a couple of days. It actually looks less nasty than it did."

She wrinkled her nose. "Disgusting."

Preech bent over and put his fingers on Ted's neck, and then on his wrist.

Ted barked out a snort.

Preech leaned back and waved his hand in front of his face. "His vitals are good but dang, the dude's toxic. Definitely should *not* be behind the wheel."

Ted snored like a hibernating bear. A long, glimmering string of drool oozed down the black and white stubble on his cheek.

"This place gives me the creeps. Let's get out of here," Tiff said.

Preech nodded. "Since I'm not exactly street legal, can't load Ted up and take him in, so I say we figure out a way to secure him here. We'll call the police and let them know where he is."

"Good thinking," I said. "I used all the itching powder on his clothes, so be careful what you touch."

He smiled. "Whoa, the whole bottle? This place will be contaminated for fifty years. Hey, would you grab me some bailing wire out of the back of the truck?"

I gathered an armload of the fist-sized wads that were like metal spaghetti and dumped them next to Preech. "And I'll take that," I said as I popped my shoe off of Ted's foot. A stench like rotten corn chips radiated out of it. I gagged so hard, it felt like my stomach wrapped around my spine.

Preech knelt next to Ted and unwound one of the balls of wire. "Hey, Miss Montana, you ever hog-tie a steer?"

"Got second place in calf-roping at our county rodeo last month."

"Why does that not surprise me... A little help here?"

I ran to the passenger door, pulled it open, and smiled at the mangled piggy bank. Not wanting to nasty up the inside of Old Betsy, I tossed my shoe in the truck bed. It landed on an old tarp, and I jumped back. Had something under it moved?

Keeping one eye on the tarp, I pulled out our lucky rocks. Sunlight bounced off all four at the same time, so bright it was hard to look directly at them. I felt each one until I knew I'd found mine. I set the rest back in the piggy bank, and then slid my little friend into my pocket.

I grabbed the corner of the tarp, about to pull it back, when Preech said, "Dude, quick, check this out."

I let go, walked towards Preech, and laughed as I passed Ted. "Dang, y'all are fast." Wire was wound around his ankles and wrists, and they were bound together, sticking straight up in the air. He looked like a big, ugly, lumpy-headed fly that had flown into a giant robot spider's web.

Preech tapped the bumper and whistled. "Metal surrenders when trees kiss fenders. Will you pull Old Betsy backwards to see if it'll stay attached?"

"Okay." I climbed into the truck. "Hey, what's under the tarp in the back?"

He shrugged. "Dunno. I bet feed or something The Oracle wants to keep dry."

Preech and Tiff stepped back. I cranked up Old Betsy, put her in "R," and stepped on the gas. The wheels spun, but nothing happened for a bit. Suddenly, a loud, groaning pop echoed through the woods as she shivered, shook, and pulled away from the trees.

Preech held up his hands. "Whoa, that's good."

I turned the truck off, got out, and helped him try to push the part of the bumper that had ripped away back into place.

He sighed. "I don't think I can fix it without Uncle Oliver's tools. We can secure it with some wire for the trip back."

Once we were done, Preech dusted off his hands. "Let's roll. I won't feel right until we call the police and get Old Betsy back home and fixed up."

We climbed in, and Preech cranked the key. I pointed at the row of letters next to the long shiny handle. "What does 'N' stand for?"

Preech snapped his fingers. "A perfect word for the day. I've named that nebulous, which means unclear or hazy, as I have yet to determine what function it serves."

I handed him the piggy bank. He fingered the lucky rocks until he found his and plucked it out. "Booyah, to the victors go the spoils. We did it, y'all; we did it!"

The three of us high-fived and hugged. Old Betsy rolled onto the blacktop, and Preech said, "I doubt The Oracle has any Queen eight-tracks in here. See if you can find 'We Are the Champions' on the radio."

I checked all six stations. "Nope." But when Jimmy Buffet's song "Cheeseburger in Paradise" came on, Preech nodded, and I cranked it up. We sang the whole way back and coasted to a stop by Oliver's house. Preech turned Old Betsy off and patted the steering wheel. "Whew, glad we had enough gas to make it." He reached out and picked at a dried bug splat with his fingernail, and then looked at us and grinned. "Do you know the last thing that goes through an insect's mind when he hits the windshield?"

"No," we said.

"His butt!"

I laughed so hard I couldn't breathe. The warm buzz growing in my stomach made me feel like I could do anything.

Curi tore around the side of the house. His paws hit the driver's side door, and the sour stink of skunk infused (one of Preech's "word for the day") the inside of the truck.

"Buddy, what were you thinking?" Preech said. He and Tiff rolled up the windows. "Smells like someone went huntin' under the barn again. We gotta tie him up, so he doesn't go inside the house and pollute everything."

I pointed at a tennis ball in the grass. "If y'all keep him busy, I'll grab some rope out of the back."

"Hey," Tiff said, "will he play fetch in the pond? You figure the water might wash some of it off?"

Preech nodded. "Good thinkin'; he loves that. His leash is inside the cabinet in the kitchen." He opened the door a crack. "Hey, boy, go get your ball."

I climbed out behind Tiff, and as I got up the porch stairs, Preech said, "Bring the leash out, and we'll tie him to a tree, then call the cops on Ted, then fix Old Betsy."

I saluted him, grabbed the leash, jumped down the porch steps, and jogged towards the pond.

Curi climbed out with the ball in his mouth. As he shook, Tiff and Preech jumped back, like the skunk stink was somehow traveling with the water drops flying off of him. Curi looked towards me and dropped the ball. The hair on his back shot up. He let out the meanest, baddest growl I'd ever heard. Preech grabbed the collar. Curi pulled so hard I thought he was going to yank Preech's arm off. "Whoa, easy!" Preech hollered.

Tiff tried to calm him down. "It's okay. You know Kevin. Everything's alright."

"Must hate the leash," Preech yelled over the high-pitched whines and yelps. He pulled Curi next to a mesquite tree. I tied the leash to it, and Preech clipped the other end to his collar.

"Poor thing. After we call the police, let's untie him and get him settled. Think he's looking for Oliver?"

"Could be." Preech sniffed his hands, grimaced, and then rubbed mud on them and wiped it on the grass to try and get the skunk smell off.

Preech and Tiff headed to the house. I stopped by Old Betsy to pat the tire on my bike. It was a little banged up, but was mine again. The puzzle pieces of my life were all falling into place. I pulled out my lucky rock. Thoughts of super-cool red cars for Mom and dolls with hair for Milly danced through my mind. I looked at my cast net, cans of food, and the other stuff slung around the back of Old Betsy. My eyes stopped on the tarp—flatter than a pancake.

"Huh," I said. "Must've been the wind."

The screen door screeched open. Preech walked out, scratched his head, and jumped off the porch.

"Hey, bud, we forgot to pick up the other bikes at Old Man Perkins'." He snapped his fingers. "Well, one more thing for the to-do list."

"What did the cops say?" I asked.

"Phone's screwed up," he said. "I called and got one ring then the line went dead. Gonna check if the wind or rain messed with it." He walked around the side of the house, and a second later came screaming back, high-stepping and waving his arms. "Snake! Big snake!"

I'd never seen him flip out like that over a snake. It had to be huge. And The Oracle had upped the bounty to two bucks for every rattle button, possibly enough to earn Preech's payback money.

I grabbed a hoe lying against the porch and ran around the side of the house. There it was, separating grass blades as it hurried out of the yard, about to disappear behind a huge oak tree. The thump of blood pumping roared in my ears as I sprinted towards it. I'd deal the beast a mighty death blow, climb the tree until it bled out, and collect my bounty when The Oracle came back. Images of Luke Skywalker's light saber slicing through the air filled my mind, but were disrupted by a sickening and familiar *click, click, click* getting louder with every step.

I jumped around the mighty oak, pulled back the hoe in full-on Jedi attack mode, and then skidded to a stop.

It wasn't a snake; it was the phone line that had been ripped away from the house.

And standing next to the telephone pole was a man pulling it. He had red hair, one handcuff, one shoe, and a wicked-evil grin.

CHAPTER 21

The man tore the hoe out of my hand, spun me around, and shoved it into my back so hard I barely kept my feet under me. "Back to the house. Now."

The dude was massive. A hot, thick, animal-like scent of sweat and body odor oozed out of him, surrounding us as we headed to Oliver's.

Preech stood next to the porch, staring at Curi, who barked, growled, and pulled against the leash so hard I thought the mesquite tree might rip out of the ground. Preech waved at us. "Howdy, neighbor, your phone out, too?" His smile slowly disintegrated, and his eyes filled with surprise as he realized what was happening.

The man pointed the hoe at Preech, then at Old Betsy, and then back at me. "You. Get that rope. Bring it here."

Preech nodded, pulled it out of the truck, and walked back to us.

The hard metal chewed into my spine. "Tie him up. Real good and tight, or I'll bury this thing six inches in his head and run the handle through you. Got it?"

I held my arms out and Preech, wide-eyed and quiet, snugly circled and knotted the rope around my wrists. Once Preech was done, the man inspected the rope handcuffs. Next, he shoved me down so hard I thought my teeth shattered when they slammed together. He stuck the hoe an inch away from Preech's face. "Turn around. Arms behind you." The man pulled a few feet of rope off and tied Preech's hands together.

He winced as the rope dug into his wrists. "Umm, sir, can I ask what you're going to do with us? Mister..."

"Name's Zeke." He knocked Preech to the ground next to me. "Try anything, and it'll be the last breath you take. Got it?"

We nodded.

Zeke cupped his hands around his mouth and yelled towards the house. "Know you're in there, chick. Phone don't work. Out here. Now."

Tiff left the house, closed the door, and wearing a terrified look, shuffled across the yard.

"Hands behind you." Zeke tied Tiff's wrists together. He pointed at the ground. "Sit. Now."

She eased down next to Preech.

Zeke walked backwards towards the house. "Better not hear a word." Wood screamed as he kicked the door open. He poked his head out of a window, pointed to his eyes, and then at us. "I'm watching you. You move, you die." He disappeared. Shattering glass pierced the still afternoon air as a chair sailed through it.

"What's he doing?" Tiff whispered.

"Maniac's trashing the place," Preech whispered back.

Zeke emerged with an armload of rifles. Oliver's pocket watch dangled from his belt loop. Tiff groaned as he opened Old Betsy's passenger door, threw the rifles onto the floorboard, and then twirled the watch in his hand. He bit it, nodded, and slipped it into his pocket.

Halfway back to the house, Zeke stopped and pointed at Curi. "Shut that fleabag up or I will. For good."

Curi barked and snapped at Zeke. Dog slobber dripped from his sharp fangs.

"It's okay, good dog. It's okay," pleaded Tiff. "Calm down, boy; please calm down."

Zeke stomped to the house. Horrible smashing noises floated out of the shattered windows. He walked out with cans of food wrapped in Oliver's Army dress greens.

After dumping everything on the floorboard, he took a sideways look at Oliver's jacket. Zeke whipped it as carelessly as somebody shaking dirt out of a rug. The shiny medals caught pieces of sunlight as they twirled off of the uniform and disappeared into the grass.

"Awful." Tiff squeezed her eyes shut. "I can't watch."

Once the jacket was stripped bare, Zeke tossed it in the truck and headed back into the house. He returned with Oliver's service pistol in one hand and a fistful of money in the other.

"He found Oliver's cash stash," whispered Preech.

Zeke set the money and pistol on the truck seat, and then pulled a wad of bills out of his pocket. As he twisted it in his hand, I noticed a Dallas Cowboys money clip that clamped the cash together, exactly like the one my grandfather had given me. Images shot lightning fast through my brain: the footprints outside Milly's window and around Old Man Perkins', and my stinky shoe when it popped off Ted's right foot. All the scenes had a shoe on the left foot and bare right foot. Just like Zeke.

Remembering what Milly said, I focused on his red hair. "It was you."

He stepped towards me, spitting through his teeth. "Me what?"

"They said there were two bodies they couldn't find. My little sister gave you my money."

Zeke slowly nodded and rubbed his chin. "I remember her. Might just pay that little blue-eyed porcupine another visit on the way out of town."

He turned to go back to the house, and that's when it happened.

First, I got a little dizzy. Curi's barks and growls drowned out, and everything around me blended into a green and brown blur. I pictured him taking Milly and imagined what he might do to Mom or Dad if they were there. The thought of him even *looking* at any of them sent a white-hot bolt of fury that started in my toes and seared through me straight to my brain. It exploded against some kind of dam that had been there forever. I shivered in the warm afternoon sunbeams as the dam crumbled. Through the massive cracks poured all the words and frustration that had bottled up for as long as I could remember.

I studied Zeke as he strutted back to the house. The dude was huge. Much bigger and meatier than Ted, and he could probably snap me in half like a crayon. But a hopeful excitement surged through me that I had words, that I had *power*.

Zeke walked out in a pair of overalls and boots, his arms wrapped around two sleeping bags, pillows, and the blanket from Oliver's bed. He threw it in the truck.

Words flew out of my mouth. "Zeke, sir, any chance I can go with you? Nothing really left for me here. My folks split up." I nodded towards Preech. "And my so-called best friend kicked me to the curb last night. If he did it once, he'll do it again, am I right?"

"Preech." Tiff huffed, a look of disgust on her face.

His head whipped back and forth from me to her. "Huge misunderstanding." Preech's voice cracked. "Dude, I thought everything was cool."

Zeke looked at us over his shoulder. "I ain't no babysitter. Probably stick y'all inside this dump before I torch it."

The next trip out, Zeke had Oliver's favorite frying pan in one hand and a box of matches in the other. Figuring he was about done packing up, I had to think fast.

"You know, Zeke, sir, they won't be looking for, say, a kid and his uncle going on a fishing trip." I smiled the biggest smile I could. "And I learned how to drive. I can take over when you get tired if you want."

He shook his head. "I saw you behind the wheel at that old shack. A blind dog could drive better than you."

I pointed my bound hands at Old Betsy. "Oh, and by the way, you aren't thinking of taking *that* truck, are you?"

"Kevin?" Tiff asked.

"Dude," Preech hissed.

I shrugged. "Not gonna go too far on a cup of gas, sir."

He opened the door and looked at the dashboard. "Tank's full."

"As they say, things aren't always as they appear. I'd check it if I were you."

Zeke's eyes turned to slits. He unscrewed the gas cap, pressed his ear against the metal under it, and rapped his knuckles down the side of Old Betsy. He stomped over next to Tiff and yanked the rope up off the ground.

She flinched as he whipped out Oliver's favorite whittling knife, flipped it open, and sliced off a few feet. Zeke took it back to the truck, fed it into the tank, pulled it out, and stared at me as he tapped the tip.

"Gas can is in the garage, sir," I said. "Should be plenty to get you to a station for a fill-up."

Curi's barks and howls grew louder as Zeke headed to the garage.

"Somebody shut that mutt up. Now!"

"Hush, boy, it'll be alright," Tiff begged. "Please calm down, okay?"

"It's Priscilla," sobbed Preech.

"What?" Tiff and I said at the same time.

"Since we're going to die today," he continued, "it's important I told my best friend and the only girl I've ever loved."

"What?" Tiff asked again, a little louder.

"My name. Either the doctor that delivered me had some sick sense of humor or was in a hurry to go to a golf match or something, but he checked the box that said 'girl' instead of the box that said 'boy.'" Preech leaned forward and did air quotes behind his back. "After they'd already named me, my folks thought it'd be 'cute' to keep it that way." He sat back, stared at me, and shrugged. The gleam in his eyes was gone, giving them a blank, hollow look, like he'd given up.

"No, hombre," I said. "We're gettin' out of this."

Zeke had found the gas can. He poured it into Old Betsy, staring at us like a crocodile eyeing three catfish on a stringer, wondering which one to eat first.

"Oh, and, Zeke, sir, did you find his super-secret hidey-hole? The one in the floorboards in his room? Where he hides the Nazi gold he brought back?"

"Duuude?" Preech wheezed.

Zeke raised his eyebrows. "Where?"

"About six paces left of his bedroom closet, two paces north, one more east."

I held up my hands. "Actually, may be easier to just show you. If you wouldn't mind untying me, I'd be more than happy to help you f—"

"Not a chance." He finished pouring the gas, tossed the empty can into the yard, and stood over me.

"Hey, while I'm thinking about it, did you know we had diamonds?" I pointed my bound hands to the lump in Preech's pocket.

His chin slumped to his chest, and he whimpered as I dug his lucky rock out and handed it to Zeke.

Zeke twirled it in his hand. "That headcase Ted wouldn't shut up about these. How many you got?"

"Four total," I said, and I held my arms up to him again. "May have to hunt them all down; would be a lot quicker if I was untied."

He shook his head. "Ain't gonna happen." Zeke went to the truck, picked up Oliver's service pistol, loaded it, and then walked back and cut through the section of rope connecting me to Preech.

He yanked me to my feet and shoved the barrel into my back. "Move. Show me the gold and the other diamonds. After that, I'm done with you."

We approached Pele's pen. My fingers frantically raked at the outside of my pants until my lucky rock finally climbed out of my pocket and into my palm. I held it up, so he could see it over my shoulder. "Here's one more, sir. And I think the other two are in the—"

Performing the best fake trip ever, I watched the muddy ground fly towards my face with one eye while the other watched my lucky rock sail through the air. With just enough topspin, it landed perfectly with a quiet muddy splat a few feet behind Pele.

"Whoops, two left feet, I guess. Little help here?" I rolled over and offered my hands to him.

Zeke rolled his eyes and slapped them aside. "Idiot."

He jammed the pistol into his pocket, climbed through the barbed wire, and bent over to pick up my lucky rock.

"Pele," I said, my voice so deep and growly I almost didn't recognize it. His ears swiveled backwards. I yelled, "Score!"

Pele wound both back legs up, and I swear he grinned as he launched his hooves into Zeke's face and hip. There was a loud, wet crunch. Zeke sailed sideways into the barbed wire. Like on Saturday night wrestling, he bounced off and staggered back towards Pele.

"Score!" I yelled again, and Pele's hooves burrowed into Zeke's face and chest.

Something whizzed past my head. A tooth maybe?

"Ooooooh," I said as Zeke did a full flip, landed in a crumpled heap next to the fence, and melted into the mud and muck.

Oliver's service pistol spun through the air. I flinched as it splatted into the mud a few feet from my head.

"Good boy, Pele. Carrots every day for you, my new hairy, muscly, beastly friend!"

"Woo-hoo!" Preech hollered. "You are the man, Kev!"

Tiff bounced up and down, her eyes wet with tears. "Thank you, thank you! Set us free, hero!"

I gnawed on my rope handcuffs until the knots loosened. They slid off, and I untied Preech. He untied Tiff, then ran to Old Betsy, grabbed an armload of baling wire, and within a couple of minutes had both of Zeke's feet bound together and his arms secured to a cedar fence post.

"Pele," I said and opened the gate on the far side of his pen. "Go out to the pasture. Go on." He stared at me. "Pasture. Now. Scoot."

Pele blinked, gave a quick nod, and eased out of his pen. I closed the gate, climbed through the barbed wire, and found my lucky rock stuck in the muck. I slipped and slid until I got next to Zeke and wiped my lucky rock off on him. He moaned as I extracted (one of Preech's "word for the day") the cash, Preech's lucky rock, and Oliver's pocket watch and whittling knife from his overalls.

Preech separated the strands of barbed wire so I could climb through. I flipped the golden watch lid open and showed it to him. "Sure glad this didn't find its way between Zeke and one of Pele's kung fu moves. That wouldn't have ended well."

Preech nodded. "You got that right."

I wrapped it in the wad of Oliver's loose bills to give back to him, and then pulled the cash out of my money clip and handed it to Preech. "All I got is twenty. I'll get you the rest as soon as I can."

"No problemo, amigo. I know you're good for it."

Preech stuffed it in his wallet. "I need to roll to the neighbors to call the police. Mind if I borrow your bike? Not exactly comfortable taking Old Betsy out of her natural habitat again."

"You go, bud. Tell them now there are two dirt bags to pick up."

We unloaded the bike, and he took off. I met Tiff at the bottom of the porch stairs, where she tied the leash to the porch railing. Curi furiously licked her hand, then whimpered and whined when he glanced at Zeke's body on the ground.

"Stay," Tiff said to Curi, and then she gasped when I pushed the broken door open with my foot. "Looks like a tornado ripped through here. How did he do so much damage so quickly? It's awful."

Everything that could have been broken was smashed beyond recognition. My heart broke for The Oracle. "I don't know where to start."

CHAPTER 22

A police cruiser showed up with two officers I'd seen before but didn't know. Not far behind it was Mr. Roman from the newspaper, then an ambulance.

Preech rolled back on my bike, parked it in the garage, and shook his head in disbelief when he saw the inside of the house. The policemen and Mr. Roman took pictures, and we answered questions about everything that had happened.

The ambulance drove away with what was left of Zeke, and a truck pulled up. Then another, and another, and soon it seemed like half the county had appeared at The Oracle's.

The sounds of banging hammers and buzzing saws soon filled the air. I knew some of the people, and some I didn't, but I recognized a lot of them as having come to The Oracle for advice on everything from ducklings with broken legs to bent-up tractor tires. If they had a problem, they'd come from miles away to talk to him and get it figured out. Since he never took a dime, I figured this was their way of repaying him.

Very cool.

I got on my hands and knees with Mr. and Mrs. Foster, who had to be like eighty, until we found all the Army medals in the grass. With the help of a picture Preech had taken of Oliver in his uniform and given him for Christmas, we pinned each one back exactly where it belonged.

People climbed all over Old Betsy, reminding me of remora fish cleaning parasites off of a shark. They got the bumper back into place, and scoured every speck of dirt and mud off of her. I laughed when I thought that some of it had been on there forever, or "since when Moby Dick was a guppy" like The Oracle sometimes said.

I smiled when I saw Priscilla—whoops, I mean Preech (a secret I would take to the grave)—sitting atop a ladder on the side of the house, the tip of his tongue stuck out and a book titled *Wire Repair* balanced on his knee.

Tiff and a group of others surrounded an old wash tub, scrubbing a very happy Curi, who was submerged in what looked like gallons of tomato juice. He slurped and bit at the gooey red liquid.

Mr. Phillips from the hardware store had Oliver's service pistol in pieces on the picnic table, cleaning and oiling everything with the care of a master watchmaker.

A siren burst jolted me out of my thoughts. Another police cruiser pulled up and parked between the rows of cars and trucks that stretched all the way to the road.

Preech appeared next to me, tool pouch in hand.

Officers Shipley and Duncan got out, and we all shook hands.

"Thank you for the tip. The fugitives have been apprehended and processed, but we've got a couple of questions."

Preech and I nodded.

Officer Duncan continued. "The perp we picked up at the Perkins' place is pretty banged up. Got hives an inch thick and wouldn't stop yapping about some kid trying to poison him with 'voodoo juice.' Any ideas about that?"

Preech looked at me, winked, and we shook our heads.

"As I recall," Officer Shipley said, "something was covered up in the little bike basket of yours that fit the dimensions of the bottle we found at the scene. Anything you want to explain before we dust for prints?"

Preech reached over, pinched my lips shut, and cleared his throat. "Umm, sirs, would it behoove my client to funnel everything through his legal representation from this moment forward?"

They grinned at each other, and then at Preech.

Officer Duncan said, "You can tell your client, due to him going above and beyond his duty as a citizen, that the particular item of interest will most likely find its way into a trash can before it gets mixed in with the rest of the evidence."

Preech nodded. "Duly noted. Thank you for your time and assistance, officers. By the way, did you have any issues apprehending him?"

Duncan shook his head. "Nope. There was about a hundred feet of baling wire keeping him in check. That your handiwork?"

Preech smiled and puffed out his chest.

"Appreciate you boys." They turned to leave.

"Excuse me, sirs," I asked, "was there anything else he said? Something about a letter, perhaps?"

Preech stiffened next to me. He whispered, "Duuude?"

I whispered back. "Sometimes, you gotta go ahead and rip the Band-Aid off. We got this."

Officer Shipley snapped his fingers and wheeled around. "That's the other thing he wouldn't shut up about. Said the 'measly, weird, pasty' kid was figuring things out. Would that be you?"

My cheeks burned. "Umm, yes, sir, I guess so. Still working on it. Can't someone get in a lot of trouble for that?"

Officer Duncan rubbed a scar on his cheek. I was pretty sure he got it the day Ted broke the officer's jaw in Rudy's backyard. "He's got a laundry list of offenses, probably about to add a few more. And the key witness he mentioned is, well..." He glanced at Officer Shipley, who nodded. "Is no longer with us," continued Officer Duncan. "He was identified as one of the crash victims. I don't see things going anywhere on that end." He tipped his hat. "If I was you, I wouldn't burn any time worrying about it."

"Way ahead of you, sir. And thank you for what y'all do," I said.

Their doors slammed shut, and their cruiser backed out of the driveway.

"Whew, glad that's over," Preech said. "Think I'm almost done with the phone line. Good thing it isn't high voltage. If it was, my hair would probably look like Ronald McDonald's by now." He jogged back to the house.

I laughed, but was interrupted by a familiar horn tap. Mom's dragon wagon pulled up. She was driving; Dad sat in the passenger seat.

Mom ran from the car and crushed me in a hug. "Your father and I just heard. Are you okay?"

I nodded, and as Dad walked next to her, he slid his hand into hers. I felt like crying, singing, and barfing all at the same time.

"Listen, Mom and Dad, nothing is so bad it can't be fixed. There's gotta be a way to make things right with you two. I'm in the bait business now, so I can pay for an old priest and a young priest or whatever we need to get everything back to normal. Separate Christmases would be horrible."

A cheesy grin slid across Dad's face, his head tilted sideways, and he stared at me like an arm had grown out of my forehead. "What on earth are you talking about?"

"Y'all divorcing. Splitting up. Taking everything away."

He laughed. "What? Buddy, your mom and I will be fine."

"Huh?"

A frown replaced his toothy smile. "Your aunt Deedee is sick...really sick. We had to sell about everything we had to help pay for her flight and treatment by a doctor in New York. They say he's the best in the world." Dad rubbed the tan line on his ring finger. "It was tough letting some things go, but it's just stuff. Maybe we'll get it

146

all back someday. Caused a bit of friction between me and your mom, but like always, we'll figure things out."

Mom sighed. "We're all Deedee's got. It's what families do. She's gonna see the best doctors. She'll be okay."

"So, y'all aren't getting divorced?"

"What?" Mom laughed. "Divorce? Honey, the guilt would kill me. You two wouldn't make it a week."

Dad and I looked at each other, shrugged, and nodded.

"Now Milly's a different story," she continued. "That kid could tame a hurricane."

We nodded harder and grinned.

Mom gripped my shoulders and stared me dead in the eyes. "Must have been terrifying thinking something so awful was going on. Why didn't you just ask us?"

Now *that* was the five-hundred-dollar question, and I didn't have an answer. But the million-dollar question was whether it would ever happen again. A soaring freedom rippled through me when the word "*No*" lit up in my head. Never again would I burn a second of fishing time, or life, without first asking the right person the right question before I decided if I needed to worry about anything, and going to the right people when I had a problem.

Would it be uncomfortable? Yep. Would I get an answer I didn't want to hear? Maybe. But I was forever okay with that.

Mom held me at arm's length and looked me up and down. "Something's different. Think you hit a growth spurt?"

I smiled. "Something like that."

CHAPTER 23

Oliver's new army worked through the night and most of the next day.

By late afternoon, Old Betsy gleamed, the inside and outside of Oliver's house sparkled, and "Curi the skunk slayer" still stunk, but not as bad.

Minutes after the last truck pulled out, Daisy's car rolled in.

Oliver pulled himself out and whistled. "From what we caught on the radio, I figured it'd look like a war zone around here, but I've never seen the place look better."

Daisy hugged me. "So grateful y'all are okay. Sounds like we get to hear about a major adventure."

I took a deep breath, trying to figure out where to begin, when Oliver's phone rang inside the house.

Preech leapt out of his chair. "It works? The phone works!" He flew off the porch and launched into his victory dance.

The Oracle hurried up the steps. "Hold that thought, Private Kevin. I don't want to miss a word."

"Mind if I join in?" I asked Preech. "Never done it before, but I sure feel like giving it a try."

He bowed and nodded. "Plenty of room, amigo. Come on."

Instead of V's in the air, my dance evolved (one of Preech's "word for the day") into more a fishing-themed dance. I twirled in circles, with my arms going back and forth like I was reeling in one whopper after another.

Rudy, Tiff, and Daisy laughed, Curi howled, and I probably looked like a carp out of water. But all I could do was dance, laugh, and howl along with them and enjoy the best feeling I'd had in a long, long time.

A few minutes later, the screen door opened so fast it almost sailed off its hinges.

We stopped dancing. "So, who was the lucky first caller on your new and improved phone line, sir?" Preech asked.

"That, my boy, was a collect call from Germany," boomed Oliver. A smile as big as Texas spread across his face. "Saddle up, posse. They found her!"

ACKNOWLEDGEMENTS

And a Texas-sized THANK YOU to all of the peeps that helped make Fishing for Luck happen in their own, special ways. In no particular order, because you can't measure awesomeness.

Mom, Jen, Annie, Max, Andrea, John, Meridith, Clay, Hans, Zion, Keaton, Amy, Trilby, Noelle, Todd, Lena, Lindsey, Knox, J.D., Bill S., Jake, Monte, Muffet, Bill B., Laney, Mary Bill, HB, Denise, Amber, Brad (HCH), Jessica, Nathan the art wizard, Dan, Nancy, Lori, Brenda, Nate, Nicole, Cade, Darron, Simone, Eddie, Christy, Erin, Aimee, Peter, Bethany, Carson, Brayden, Ramirezstein, Russell, Shay (my Alvarado NOF), DPL librarians (the most helpful literary Sherpas on the planet), Anthony, Amanda, Catie, Jennifer K., Toni, Jake (please check out and support *Angling for Relief* – good people doing great things to help pediatric cancer patients), Stephanie, Whitney, Michael, Angela, Bryan, Anita, Dennis, Libby, Madi, Misty, Emil, Leah, Brian, Dr. Scot, Brian O., Brett, Sgt. Bradshaw, Beth B., Juli, Austin, Dan, Pat, Finley, Liliana, Mindy, Anna, William, Judi, Gabbie, Ethan, Anderson, Joanne, TC, MS, Dietrich, and McLennan County's best and brightest – Mindy, Ann, Amanda, Tonya, Angie, Kristine, Angela, and Delaney Rose.

ABOUT THE AUTHOR

From the first second I held a fishing pole, I was hooked. To this day, I can't pass a body of water without wondering what kind of fish (or bait) are cruising around in it. I also love a good joke, and playing jokes on people—which is why I rarely answer my phone or open email around April Fool's day!

I graduated from the University of Texas with a degree in Journalism, and once heard a really smart person say "Readers are Leaders." I hope you agree.

Please visit my website at www.murrayrichter.com.

A NOTE ABOUT REVIEWS

Reviews help books find readers. They are like gold for some authors (more like reeling in a keeper crappie for me), so would you, together with your parent or guardian, be so kind as to leave one on Amazon, Goodreads, or the platform of your choice? When you do, somebody, somewhere in the world, will catch a fish.

Thank you, and all the best,

Murray

Made in the USA
Columbia, SC
29 June 2021